D0425991

DATE DUE   2/15-

MAY 1 2 2015	
SEP 1 9 2015	
JAN 2 4 2018	
APR 1 0 2018	
	DISCARD
	PRINTED IN U.S.A.

Snow

Calvin Miller

Snow

A Novel

BETHANY HOUSE PUBLISHERS
MINNEAPOLIS, MINNESOTA 55438

Published by Bethany House Publishers
A Ministry of Bethany Fellowship International
11300 Hampshire Avenue South
Minneapolis, Minnesota 55438
www.bethanyhouse.com

Printed in the United States of America by
Bethany Press International, Minneapolis, Minnesota 55438

ISBN 0-7642-2152-3

To

Melanie

CALVIN MILLER is a poet, pastor, theologian, painter, and the writer of over thirty books. His writing spans a wide spectrum of genres, from the bestselling SINGER TRILOGY to *The Book of Jesus*. He presently serves as Professor of Communication and Ministry Studies at Southwestern Baptist Theological Seminary.

To begin with, it was the winter of '29—an ordinary winter, with no hint of miracles in the slate skies over King of Prussia, Pennsylvania. *The Farmer's Almanac*, called *The Witches' Book* by the modest Amish, predicted snow. The air was moistly eager for such a white prediction. It was cold, too, though not excessively. The air was biting, but one could stand it. Union strikes and layoffs had left the coal mines of Appalachia very quiet. Much of Pennsylvania and most of New England doubted there would be enough coal to last the winter. But on this particular December evening it was the shortage of daylight, not coal, that troubled most Pennsylvanians.

Mary Withers dreaded December because the sun rose so late and stayed so far away. The Atlantic Ocean, of course, was the real culprit. It was an odd paradox that the humid ocean air could produce such deep snow. But every time the warm, capricious air of the Atlantic met arctic moisture, winter storms buried Eastern Pennsylvania in white. Some said that the ocean and *The Farmer's Almanac* were in cahoots. What the *Almanac* predicted, the Atlantic had sworn to back up. But Mary agreed with the Amish about *The Farmer's Almanac*. It was indeed *The Witches' Book*. Yet she well knew that the witches of winter sometimes dressed in white.

Mary wasn't altogether sure that anyone could predict the weather. It had a mind of its own. And this year it seemed determined to give the children of King of Prussia a gift that even Santa could not give them. Mary could tell the weather was going to change, because the sun was circled by misty rings. That's how every big snow announced its coming: it beguiled the cowardly sun. Soon the sickly December daylight would pile the early evening shadows full of white formality.

It's neither Almanac *nor witches*, said Mary to herself. *It snows by general consensus. Sometimes it simply must snow because everyone knows it will.* The local bakery had stacked bread to towering heights in the windows. *It is a sign*, thought Mary. And every house had laid by a mountain of coal. This, too, was a sign—all were agreed. Everyone knew it: snow was on the way. Public opinion would have it no other way. Those who wanted it were anxious; those who didn't were nervous. Mary Withers was neither nervous nor anxious. It was two weeks until the holidays, and she had work to do.

She donned her felted bonnet, grabbed the hatchet from the back porch, and stepped out into the cheerless morning. She didn't hesitate. She had made her selection in August. Walking directly to the thin spruce at the back of her three-acre lot, she stopped and studied the tree. *How thin you are*, thought Mary to herself, *the perfect symbol for a needy Christmas. You are not much of a tree but big enough, I think, to support two strands of lacquered cranberries and a thin thread of popcorn.* Mary knew her small hatchet was dull, so she expected the green and willowy spruce to fall with some reluctance. The hatchet bounced against the spongy bark several times before the tree began to yield. Mary swung ever harder, hacking at the thin trunk just above the frozen ground. The tree was willowy enough to challenge both the hatchet and Mary. But unsteadily holding on to life, the tree at last yielded to the flying green and gold chips that set it free of its roots.

Dragging the tree behind her, Mary turned toward the house. There was no chance the tree would pick up dust. The ground was too frozen for that. In but a brisk two minutes she was at her own back porch. She ferreted an old bucket from under the rear stoop. It was filled with last year's sand, which had remained dry enough not to freeze. She carried the tree inside and placed it upright in the sand, and there the small green tree at last acquired a kind of royalty. *Tannenbaum* it wasn't. Yet reeking of its own glorious resin, it bestowed a kind of incense never swung from the bishop's censer in the cathedrals of New York.

Mary had exactly seven glass ornaments. When she and Tom were first married, she had owned a dozen. But some of the spring clips that held the top of the balls to their delicate globes were tired. These weaker clips had through the years just given out, dropping their fragile spheres to the oak floor that destroyed them. Mary would hang them all in the front of the tree, giving the false impression that there were surely seven more on the reverse side.

Something new was to be added this Christmas. She and Alexis, her six-year-old daughter, had trimmed the unprinted margins of old newspapers and cut them into three-inch strips. They used flour paste to form the strips into interlocking paper rings. This broad white laurel had become a garland of paper some twelve feet long. It would take its place with the old popcorn and the cranberries.

The spindling tree was thin, but thick enough to welcome Christmas to the Witherses' home. Alexis's eyes were alive. They sparkled with the joy of knowing that the Christmas tree was finally in the house.

"Now can we get out Joseph and Mary and the baby Jesus and the two wise men?" the child asked, wiggling excitedly. The question had so much energy, it was impossible for Alexis to stand still even as she asked it.

"Later, after we decorate the tree," said Mary. Mary was always amused by the fact that the child seemed not to know there should be three wise men. But Balthasar, like the five unlucky ornaments, had also succumbed to the oak floor. Mary never had the heart to tell Alexis about Balthasar. Caspar was an amputee, having lost a hand one nameless Christmas. Only Melchior was whole and very adoring in his own cheap plaster way. But Mary's depleted nativity set delighted Alexis, and that was what really mattered. Mary, who had managed to keep both herself and Alexis alive by her wit and thrift, also liked the nativity set. It was resourceful, like a Christmas play with a small cast. It just went to show that two wise men could do the work of three when they had to.

Scarcely a mile from the little room where Alexis circled the branches of the tree with cran-

13

berries, Ingrid Mueller carefully opened the wood box her grandmother had bought in Bavaria in the nineteenth century. The Steuben crystal ornaments snuggled into three ranks of red velvet. A third of them were egg shaped, a third were round, and a third were teardrops of cut prisms. The glass was heavy and very hard to break. Thus the ornaments were complete, as many in number as they had been the day her grandmother had bought them. One of them had a slight crack, but the crack was never noticed. The flawed glass ornament had never failed to reflect the candle fire.

Beneath the huge box of glass ornaments, another box housed a nativity set. It was fine Spanish porcelain, and none of the characters had ever been injured. There were three wise men—all well rested from their twelve-month vacation in plush kapok. Oh, were these wise men proud! Not one of them was an amputee.

Ingrid Mueller loved ritual and tradition. She always packed the nativity so that unpacking it would draw the characters out in a celebrative arrangement. The animals came first, next the shepherds, and finally the wise men. Only when the first part had been unpacked did the holy family come. And then the wise men knew they must adore the little blue peasant mother who had finally arrived. The wise men never failed to begin their adoration the moment the porcelain virgin was out of her box.

The final box contained a small wooden chest that held twenty-four bone-china limb clips. These beautiful holders would set the tree ablaze with light. They were each ready to receive the four-inch candles that her son Erick had brought from the five-and-dime store just that morning.

For only two dollars, Ingrid had bought a thick white pine from her cousin who owned a tree farm west of the city. Now the pine stood ready for its burdensome work of holding the heavy glass ornaments and sturdy candle clips. Still, it was a thickly foliaged tree, well able to carry any weight that Ingrid Mueller might ask it to bear.

Ingrid's husband, Hans, had been watching her lay out all of the decorations and could not help but measure her delight. Ordinarily he would not have been home for this annual ritual, but he had injured his back and was unable to work. He was a coal vendor, but this ailment had forced him to stay at home while his son Erick made the December deliveries to make sure his best customers had enough coal for the holidays.

Mary Withers and Ingrid Mueller were not in the same social circles and had never enjoyed each other's friendship. They knew each other casually at the Lutheran church, but their lifestyles were vastly different.

While Mary Withers was deciding that the coming storm was to be blamed on the weather's own mind and on public opinion, the Muellers had their own two sources of local forecasting: Ingrid's intuition and Hans' arthritis.

"It vill snow today, you know, Ingrid!" said Hans Mueller in his German accent.

"And who made you a prophet?" Ingrid asked.

"First of all, *The Farmer's Almanac* says snow."

"The *Almanac*? The book is wrong more than it's right!"

"Well, if you can't believe the book, then trust my arthritis. It is never wrong, Ingrid. My wrists are so stiff, I can hardly move 'em. And vhen my wrists are stiff, it always rains or snows. Since it is too cold for rain, I tell you it vill snow. And the ache is very bad, so I can tell you it is going to be a big snow."

Thus from Hans Mueller's arthritis came the most incontrovertible source of forecasting the weather. "Mark my vord, Ingrid . . . snow!" Hans made it clear that when the snow appeared, he should have the credit for the forecast.

Ingrid believed, but it was not because of either Hans' arthritis or the *Almanac*. How did she know? Well, she just knew. Intuition. Yes, that was it, snow by intuition. Sometimes what you feel on the inside is what happens on the outside.

Mary Withers knew that snow was easier to predict than her daughter's next attack of asthma. Whenever that ordeal came, she knew she would need Dr. Drummond's help. She therefore dreaded the coming snow, because it might hinder the doctor from getting to her house if Alexis should need him.

But Alexis held no resentment toward the forecast. What child was ever so sick she despised snow? The snow that Mary dreaded, Alexis prayed for. Alexis Withers was overjoyed at taking her sixth turn at December. Her mother, on the other hand, inwardly cringed before the task of nursing her through another winter. She had been sick so often in her brief six years of life. Yet Alexis kept a brightness in her eyes that refused to be dulled by the pain that often racked her enthusiastic, tiny body. She stood looking fixedly out of the window and tossed her chatter motherward.

"Mama," said Alexis with her nose nearly on the cold glass, "can I go out and play with Caspian?"

Her question was clever and devious. Caspian, her big Persian cat, was always dressed for arctic weather but had not the slightest desire to go out and play. Caspian preferred to keep his December place close to the potbellied stove.

"Please, Mama, I'll bundle up!"

Mary Withers' cocked eyebrow answered. "When the weather is warmer and your cold is better!"

"Please, Mama, I'll wear my mittens and corduroys," Alexis begged, though knowing her mother would not be turned. "Caspian," she turned to look at the immobile fur ball curled on the hoop-braided rug, "why don't you ever want to go out and play? You're a bad, lazy kitty." Other than casually sweeping his tail from the right to the left, Caspian made no response. Alexis turned from the window and began to play with some crayons and an old newspaper.

Mary studied her daughter. The bright-eyed child was good at creating her own diversions. She drew, as if compelled, on the newsprint. Mary felt good that she had saved a few pennies to buy her a real coloring book for Christmas. Coloring books were in as short supply as Mary's relief checks. And Alexis's sickness had nibbled at their frail income with costly medicines and doctor's calls. Mary didn't dare think about it for long. Tears were always right behind her resolve, and she had determined to keep Alexis's tenuous life as free of a weeping mother as she could. The long December nights when Alexis wasn't coughing would leave Mary time enough to cry.

She continued to stitch a mend into a pair of her old gloves. They looked as though they could not possibly last through one more cold spell, but they would have to. Mary had noticed an overlarge hole near the thumb of her right glove when she was laying a wreath on Tom's grave. That very morning she had made her annual December pilgrimage to the cemetery. Tom had been gone for three years now, yet the very thought of him warmed the air around her. Tom had known how to keep Christmas and had never failed to draw from his resourcefulness some wonderful gifts for her and Alexis, the two special women in his life. The years of their early marriage had been lean, but never Tom's spirit. There were still times when her unwillingness to let him go filled her day with friendly ghosts. At such times she fully expected to see him coming home from work, sauntering in his boyish way around the front hedge, tossing one of his wonderful grins at her. She knew he was gone, and yet their brief years together were a gift that could never be taken away from her.

She hadn't thought much about marrying again. The roguish paragon who held the throne of her heart was still too much in charge of her soul to allow her to notice anyone else. The demands of Alexis's illness provoked such a focus in Mary's life that she had no time either to seek or to be discovered by other men. Tom had told her at least once every day that she was pretty. His unfailing insistence on the subject of her beauty had convinced her. But three years had passed since Tom's bright compliments had been the mirror to her self-esteem. Now the more honest mirror at her dressing table had grown stern in its reprimand of her thin face and pale blue eyes.

She now believed that Tom had been wrong all along. She was not pretty. Not that it troubled her much. Pretty was an unnecessary idea. It could make her neither a good mother nor a good nurse, and Mary had too much to do to consume herself with such introspective evaluation. She knew that both conceit and self-censure were but ego fondling itself. *Pretty is as pretty does*, she reminded herself. *"Pretty is the most arrogant of virtues and useless where there is need in the world,"* her mother had once told her. *"Service, not vanity, is what God requires,"* her Amish grandmother had told her. Each day handed Mary Withers a stern agenda which forced her to trade her self-regard for duty. And duty had owned the last three difficult years of her life.

But she had one glorious reason to live: Alexis. Having conquered her need for personal compliment, she had taken up Tom's custom of telling the child—at least once a day—that she was beautiful. It was not a lie. Alexis was indeed beautiful. And the compliment gave the child hope that she would one day be well, and that hope gave Mary a reason to get out of bed every morning.

She lived to herself—a lot. She talked to Alexis and loved the conversations. But her mind was a treasure house of old reveries that took their life from Mary's simple trek to a tombstone set in frozen ground. Within such seclusion, Mary was able to draw strength for the hard times. So reverie, not beauty, was God's special gift to Mary Withers—at least that's how she saw things. She drifted in a warm and willing fog of bliss to that winter morn when the sun wore halos of mist and her thin tree yielded to her hatchet. Suddenly her memories were shattered like thin ice on warm glass when a swift knock sounded at the door.

Mary had been so preoccupied, she had not even noticed the noise of a truck pulling up in front of her house.

"It's Mr. Mueller's coal truck!" shouted little Alexis without even looking out the window. Alexis didn't have to look out. Mr. Mueller's coal truck was the only truck that ever came up

21

the narrow gravel road that led to their house.

"Yes, of course it is," said Mary. She stood methodically, putting down her mending in the chair she had just vacated. The knock rattled a second time. "Coming, coming!" shouted Mary, quickening her step just a little. Unhesitatingly she threw open the door. "Good morning, Mr. Mueller!"

Only it wasn't Mr. Mueller.

A much younger man stood in the doorway. His face was red, whether from the cold or from the embarrassment of not being Mr. Mueller, Mary couldn't tell.

"I'm sorry," said the young man. "My name's Erick … Erick Mueller. My father's down with a bad back, and I'm doing the coal run for him today. I don't think we've met. Are you new to King of Prussia?"

Mary smiled. "I was seven years ago. But I suppose you've been off at the university the whole time. I know your parents, though. They're always at church."

Mary stopped for a moment. The flood of conversation had suddenly evaporated. Expecting old Mr. Mueller, she was nonplussed by finding young Mr. Mueller framed in her doorway. His red-checkered mackinaw was smudged with his temporary trade. Coal dust coated his bare hands. Those gloveless hands ended in long fingers a little too pink for doing the rough work his father customarily did.

Mary looked at his hands so long that the young man smiled self-consciously and began babbling. "I'm a tenderfoot when it comes to hard work, ma'am. I teach mathematics at the university over in Syracuse. But school's out till January, and as I said, Papa's down in the back, so I'm doing the coal run today! It's hard work, but Papa did it to get me through college, so I guess I can do it for him for a week or so till he's better."

He smiled again.

He was a contradiction in his black stocking cap and smudged clothes. Tall and musta-chioed, he kept his deep blue eyes safe within the circular gold rims of his spectacles, which were beginning to fog up from the warm air that flooded out of the Witherses' doorway. *Yes, a contradiction*, Mary thought. *A professor working on a coal truck.* Mary smiled. "Well, Erick Mueller, I need only a little coal. Can I buy an eighth of a ton?"

"Sure," he said, appearing to see nothing un-usual in the small order.

Mary was certain he was trying to make her not feel bad because she had so little money. He smiled so broadly and so cheerfully that Mary almost blushed. She knew what Erick Mueller's father would have said: "Lady, we don't sell coal by the ounce!"

"May I have the key to the coal bin?" asked Erick.

Mary replied by walking to the side of the mantel where the key hung on a small brad. She took it from the hook, returned to him, and held out the key, which he accepted with a weak smile.

Mary watched and listened as he awkwardly shuffled from the steps along the walk toward the side of the house. She heard the familiar metallic thumping of coal chunks into the tin-lined bin. It was a small order and soon delivered.

Mary met him at the door within a matter of ten minutes with the money she had carefully measured.

"Thank you, Mr. Mueller," she offered as she dropped the money from her hand into his.

For one small moment their hands touched. Mary knew the touch registered no emotion for Erick, but the odd feeling of being touched by a man caused her to deposit the money in his hand swiftly and withdraw her own, letting it fall respectfully to her side.

"It's going to snow, you know, Mrs. Withers," Erick said.

Mary knew. Everyone knew.

"That eighth ton won't last too long in the kind of weather that's coming," he said.

Mary knew he was right, but if the coal could

last a week or two, that would be the time to deal with the crisis.

"Thank you, Mr. Mueller," she said.

It was the kind of "thank-you" that suggested the next word might be "good-bye."

But "good-bye" was not to be the next word.

"You can call me Erick," said the coal man.

"All right, then, Erick, thank you!"

"May I call you Mary?"

Mary's face reddened. She felt it and was sure Erick could see it. "No, Mrs. Withers will be fine. It was my late husband's name, you know. He gave it to me—I've treasured it as much since his passing as before."

"I understand," said Erick.

Mary knew he did.

"Good-bye, Mrs. Withers," said Erick.

"Good-bye, Erick."

The young coal man walked to his truck, climbed in, and turned the key in the ignition.

He smiled and waved, then drove away. His smile was warmer than the pale sun. Mary framed it in her mind and carried the picture back into the house. Once inside she looked up and saw Tom's picture looking down at her from the mantel. She felt the chill of an odd contradiction. For the first time in several years, she looked at the picture of Tom and then moved her inner eye to the vivid picture of a man smiling at her from the window of a coal truck.

She felt guilty.

Tom's face had been the only picture in her mental gallery. Now there were two. She rebuked her inner heart and quickly removed the newer picture from her mind. Once again Tom's picture stood alone.

There, she thought, *the coal man is gone.*

And he was. But three more times that day the newer picture came back, and just as many times Mary frantically removed it.

Erick Mueller means nothing to me, she argued with herself. But she was not as convincing as she wanted to be.

At six o'clock the snow began to fall. Large white flakes that destroyed distance and shut every home into its own isolated yard.

White, white, white.

December was so young that it was impossible to forecast how much snow might lie ahead in the cold winter.

Fencerows half disappeared.

Evergreens snuggled down in the white.

And King of Prussia, Pennsylvania, dressed formally for winter.

The snow fell every day for two weeks.

It was a gentle and large-flaked snow. Silently, steadily it fell. December's crystal hung from every eave, and light slid from every icy window ledge and lost itself in unrelenting flurries.

And it was very cold.

It was the cold that thwarted Mary's intention to ration her coal. The bin was empty, and so with reluctance she phoned the Muellers to order more coal. It was the older Mr. Mueller who answered. "*Ja! Ja!* I'll send Erick by . . . how's your driveway?"

"Well, I've shoveled it back a bit. The mailman's been getting in just fine!" said Mary. "I don't think Mr. Mueller will have any trouble getting up to the house."

"Well, I hope not," Mr. Mueller humphed.

Mary wished Hans Mueller wasn't so abrupt.

"We're going to have a lot more snow, you

27

know, Mrs. Withers. Better order more than an eighth of a ton. If the miner's strike continues, there might not be any coal in February—better stock up."

"All I need is an eighth of a ton," said Mary forcefully.

"All right then, good-bye," said Hans Mueller.

After Mary heard the click of the phone back in the cradle, she hung up.

She looked out the window. The sky was gray—really gray—no sun at all.

Somehow she felt that the snow they had just encountered was but a forecast of the storm about to settle upon them.

The house felt cold.

Mary was completely out of coal.

She thought Erick would likely come late, leaving her house without warmth for the whole day.

Mary's house was Tom's last legacy, paid for by a modest insurance policy, the premiums of which Tom had miraculously kept current in spite of their meager earnings. Tom had bought the insurance only a few months before he fell through the ice while ice fishing.

Mary's fears that Erick would come late were unfounded. Within the hour she heard the coal truck rattle into her driveway. She flew to the door and threw it open. Once again as she stood there waiting, Erick smiled at her from the window of his truck, beaming like a boy getting his first sled.

Stop that! she thought to herself but shouted to Erick through the open doorway, "I'm glad you've come early. I'm out—the bin is empty."

He swung down out of the truck and ambled toward her, still smiling.

For two weeks she had carried the coal from her basement to her parlor but never without seeing his warm, contagious smile. Now her two-week-old image of the smiling coal man was instantly reinforced with new warmth.

Mary shouted inwardly, *Quit that, Erick, do you hear me? You've no right to smile that way. It upsets me. I'm a widow, you know—the widow Withers.*

While she rebuked him inwardly, outwardly she said, "Look at that sky! It's going to snow again, Mr. Mueller."

"It's going to snow, *Erick*," he corrected. "I'm Erick, you're Mrs. Withers, remember?"

Mary smiled, remembering her former protest.

As she looked at young Mueller's face, she thought of Tom, and the mental pictures merged. She made an instant appraisal of the young deliveryman: *He is handsome.* Right after her silent evaluation, she felt a surge of guilt. It was the umpteenth time she had thought about

29

Erick in the last two weeks. More guilt. She blushed and looked away. Fortunately the steam had so coated the young professor's spectacles that she hoped he didn't see.

"Well . . ." said Erick, holding out his hand.

"Well, what?" replied Mary a little abruptly.

"Well, do I get the key to the coal bin or not?"

Mary turned and hurried to the corner shelf and took the key off its tiny brass hook. She promptly returned, determined not to look Erick in the eyes. She would have kept this inner pledge except that Erick's bare hand touched her own as the key passed between them. He closed his hand too suddenly around both the key and her hand, then instantly let go.

The key fell from her hand.

They both knelt to pick it up, and in trying to grab it from the threshold of the door, each clumsily clawed at the other's hand. In the end Erick won out, touching her hand a second time. That touch tingled like the weak current of the telephone magneto.

Mary had a second visitation of redness. This time Mary sensed Erick felt it too. This time also their faces were close, very close. Their eyes were so near that the simple key exchange seemed too searching, too inviting, too threatening, too everything. Quickly they dropped each other's hand and stood.

"*Farmer's Almanac* says we're in for snow

again tonight," said Erick, nervously clearing his throat and starching his spine in the attempt to drain the heat from the front of his face.

"It's witches' stuff!"

"You must be Amish?"

"My grandmother was, and she was better than the *Almanac* at predicting the weather. Still, the *Almanac* could be right on this one. The last two weeks have been brutal. It sure does feel like more snow, and that sky looks like it's just waitin' to dump it on King of Prussia."

"My, my! Mary Withers doesn't believe in the *Almanac*. Don't tell my father. He'd consider that a kind of blasphemy. Probably slight you on your next order of coal."

"Now admit it, Mr. Mueller ... er, Erick ... the witches are wrong more than they're right. The last snow they predicted failed to come. The day was so warm the groundhogs were out looking for spring." Mary realized what an odd and serious direction the conversation had taken, and she smiled a little. Then she smiled broadly. Then she laughed out loud.

So did the young Mr. Mueller. "Anyway, you'd best not let my papa hear you blaspheme either one of the two good books. He says the Bible's here to show us how to serve the Lord, and the *Almanac*'s here to show us the kind of weather the Lord's going to give us while we do the serving. Those clouds in the northwest sure do look like they're getting ready to back the *Almanac*."

"I do hope the *Almanac*'s wrong, Mr. Mueller. We've had so much winter already, and snow brings the dampness that is so hard on my little Alexis."

"Papa always says that the Lord gave us coal to keep away sickness. Coal is Papa's answer to everything. Still, if the recipe for health is a warm house, I'd better get the coal in the bin so you can have just that, Mrs. Withers." He was trying to be formal enough in his speech so that everything that had just looked haphazardly intimate could be ordered into remote propriety.

When he turned away, he smiled as though some very pleasant notion had been born in his mind. She smiled, too, not because she thought anything of the awkward exchange but because she felt good about Erick. After a moment a frowning grimace crossed her face. She felt bad that she had just felt good. She wished she had not been so cordial. Since Tom's death, Alexis had been her only focus. Erick's warm entrance to her life seemed to require a focus of its own.

In a moment the sound of a broad shovel scooping the coal from the bed of the rusty truck interrupted the still morning. The rumble of coal falling into the bin added to the refrain. The scraping and thumping noises continued for a long time. Then suddenly they stopped.

Erick returned the key—this time without incident. He smiled and thanked her for her business. She gave him the three dollars she had saved for the coal, and the truck drove away. Later in the day Mary went downstairs to get a scuttle of coal. When she opened the door to the bin, she gasped. Had Erick misunderstood her? There appeared to be more than a half ton of coal in the bin. It had been several winters since she had been able to afford so much at once. She had the odd sensation of being rich or at least middle class. The black abundance made Erick seem like a kind of ebony Midas touching her life with practical gold. Erick had come to the needy house of a widow and left it in substance.

But it wasn't the coal that was her only gift on that ordinary December day. It was the touch of a young man's hand. Nor could she drive from her mind that pair of eyes so blue they were unable to hide themselves behind a pair of steamy spectacles. How could she be thinking like this? Hadn't she just taken a small wreath to her late husband's grave? She was troubled by her hypocrisy. Once more she quarreled with her soul for even thinking of the dustman's eyes. Immediately she determined not to think any more about the coal man and his kindness. Certainly she would not think of his eyes. There was guilt in that kind of thinking. So she thought of other things. She thought of Tom out of duty. She thought of Alexis out of necessity. She thought of the coming snow out of fear. But her mind was a traitor, and before she could rebuke it, she thought of blue eyes set in gold-rimmed frames. What was this? She was usually firm in telling her mind what to think. But it was no use this time.

She thought of Erick . . . and of Erick . . . and of Erick.

"Erick, come sit by the fire." Ingrid Mueller was not really being presumptuous in uttering such an invitation merely on hearing the door slam and footfalls in the entry. She didn't need to look around. She could tell by the way he walked that it was her son. She was, of course, right. It was Erick.

"What if it isn't Erick? What if it's the Philadelphia Ripper?" laughed her coal-smudged son.

"The Philadelphia Ripper wouldn't be as likely to show up at mealtime as you are, and he'd probably eat a lot less." Ingrid grinned.

"That's probably because ripping isn't as strenuous as shoveling coal." Erick approached her menacingly, like a scholarly, bespectacled ripper, and once more he laughed. Then he picked his mother up and swung her about the room.

"Go on ... put me down. You're all sooty! Hans, tell him to put me down!" Ingrid first commanded Erick and then her husband.

Hans rose on one elbow from his temporary sickbed made from the family sofa. "I've never been able to tell him a thing, Ingrid. He's alvays been vild and wiolent," Hans offered in his thick Germanic English. Hans Mueller was a stout man whose round chest provided ample support for his sagging triple chin. He wore much heavier spectacles than his son did, and his hair had retreated to well past the crown of his head. Nonetheless, his face was cheery, as dimpled and red as Kris Kringle. "If my back vere better I'd give you a vallop you'd not soon forget, boy. Now put your mother down."

Erick obeyed.

Popping him playfully on the chest, Ingrid chided, "Could any ripper be more brutal?"

Erick ignored her, turning to his father instead. "Papa, delivering coal is hard work. Hurry up and get well."

"Now you see, boy, vhat your papa had to do to get you through that fancy-pants uniwersity."

Erick grinned and headed for the bathroom to get cleaned up for dinner.

"Before you take a shower, Erick, put the snow scoops on the front porch. You're going to need them by morning."

"Yes, Papa," Erick responded.

Erick diverted his path from the bathroom toward the back door. Deciding to move quickly rather than put on a coat, he hurried out. Without breaking his lanky strides, he grabbed the scoops from the back stoop and moved around the outside of the house toward the front. Ingrid saw him pass the window and, like many a mother, congratulated herself that she had given him to the world. After he deposited the scoops on the front porch as Hans had instructed, he reentered the house and went to shower. Soon Ingrid heard the water running and was delighted that in a short while they would all be enjoying an early dinner together.

At Hans' reference to the coming snow, Ingrid's thoughts went back to the winter of 1911, eighteen years earlier. Her mind picked a specific memory and indulged itself. The war that had taken their son Otto forever from their lives was still years away. Hans had played incessantly with his sons back then. Ingrid remembered how suddenly the snow had come that year and how excitedly her two small boys had greeted it. But what she would never forget was the wonderful snowball fight all four of them had enjoyed in their own front yard on that long-ago Christmas Eve.

It had all started when Ingrid had decided to go out and get the mail. She had walked to the mailbox, even though knowing there was not a chance the postman had managed to deliver the mail. On her return she turned awkwardly in the deep snow and began stepping as high as she could to step over the high drifts. But alas, she was too short to step high enough. She slipped on the front walk and fell into a large drift in front of the house. Inside, Otto and Erick, then nine and twelve years old, watched her fall. Then, mischievous as they were, they bolted out of the house and playfully jumped on her, holding her down in a kind of wrestling match. They were not grown, yet she could not find the footing to get up again. And each time she tried, she fell once again, much to their delight.

She called to her husband. "Hans! Hans! Make Otto and Erick behave. They won't let me up."

Hans, hearing her distress call through the open door, had come running out to rescue her from her impish offspring. "Vhat's this! You two big lugs von't let your mother up? Vhat kind of boys have I raised, anyvay? Get up! Get off! I'll vhip you two like I vhip Pilate vhen he's so interested in getting back to the shed he can't do his vork."

Pilate was the old horse that had pulled the coal wagon when the boys were smaller. How they loved the huge and gentle Clydesdale. Back then Pilate was so much a part of the family that life often revolved around him. *How is Pilate eating? How is Pilate feeling? Are there enough oats in the granary?* Pilate was often the sole object of their concern. By the time the horse died, Hans had saved enough money to buy his first truck.

"You vorthless boys!" Hans had shouted. Then just as Hans reached down to grab Otto by the nape of his neck, he, too, slipped, falling headlong into the drift with them. Ingrid could not help laughing at her husband's inglorious tumble that had left him flat on his back in the snow with his boys tumbling in on top of him. Soon everyone was throwing snow. But throwing it was too haphazard for Otto and Erick. The two boys took their hands and began filling them with snow and dumping the icy, wet handfuls down their dad's collar. He returned the favor, until all the Muellers were laughing and hurling snow at each other at very close range. How wonderful! How mean! How glorious! How mischievously Christmas—to be an entire family having a wonderful time rolling in the snow of their own front yard.

Suddenly Ingrid's memories of 1911 were shattered and 1929 returned as Erick entered the room.

"I'm here, let's eat!" he said. It was dinnertime. It had taken only a quarter of an hour, but he was so free of coal dust that his previously smudged face was now as pink as his hands. Erick eagerly took his chair, driven by the hunger of a day's hard work. Hans, supporting his round back with a pudgy hand, rose slowly from the couch. It was he who expended the most effort in getting to the dining room table. But it was clear that he was feeling better all the time. When they were all sitting at the table, Erick picked up the bread basket, instinctively reaching for a bun. As he grabbed the roll in his thin fingers, his father's heavy slap knocked the roll back into the basket.

"Ah, ah, ah! Maybe you intellectuals at the uniwersity don't pray, Erick, but God is still the giver of our feast."

Erick drew back his reach, letting the bread basket alone until the old man's religious ritual could be tended.

"*Fader*, we thank you—at least most of us thank you—for all you give us. Help the vinter to be cold so that people vill buy lots of coal that ve may experience even more of your bounty. Amen."

"Amen," agreed Erick, ignoring the capitalist ring of his father's prayer.

"Amen," agreed Ingrid, eager for Erick to taste the bread that she had made especially for him.

"I can tell you this, son, ve don't eat this vell till you come home. Your mother loves her son vith better rolls than she ever loves your poor father."

They all laughed.

"Mama," said Erick, "That Withers woman—"

"Oh, so that's vere you been—vith der black vidow of the county. You be careful of the vidows, Erick. Dey look sveet but dey spin vebs that snare the liddle professors, *ja?*"

"Now, Papa, I'm talkin' to Mama."

"So your old fader can't listen in?"

"You can listen but not comment," he said curtly to Hans before turning again in his mother's direction. "She's pretty, don't you think, Mama?"

"She's pretty poor, boy," Hans answered. "She's got a sick baby too. I'd adwise to find you a voman at the uniwersity. You didn't give her any more coal than she actually paid for, did you, boy?"

"Maybe a little," said Erick, uncomfortable with his father's intrusion into the conversation he was trying to have with his mother.

"A little. A little. Whose coal is it anyvay, Erick? I'll tell you this, boy, the quickest vay to a vidow's heart is through her coal bin."

"It's 1929, Papa. Life is hard." He paused and turned to his mother again. "Mama, do you think she's pretty or not?"

"Pretty, pretty? A hunting dog in a covey of quail is pretty. . . ."

"Hans!" Ingrid said his name loudly. She never told him to be quiet when she was ready to state her own opinion. She just said his name with extra volume. He quieted down. "Do you know, son, I've never thought much about how she looks, but she's pretty as an angel in the way she handles the adversity of life. Her little Alexis had such a bout with her asthma last month that Dr. Drummond said she wouldn't live. But two weeks later both Mary and Alexis were back in church."

"Mama, I found myself touched by her . . . well . . . by her courage. It's a courage that sticks out all over her, but I don't think she sees it. She has little money, yet she seems to live with a spirit of gratitude. I have never seen anyone who takes life sixty seconds at a time and gives thanks that for the present moment life is good. But, Mama, today we talked, only for a moment, yet it seemed a conversation I'd waited all my life to have."

Ingrid smiled and reached out and touched Erick. She understood.

"Mama, I had the oddest sensation when I saw her today," Erick went on. "It was as though I had never seen her before . . . as though I was seeing her for the first time, and that I liked what I saw."

"I gotta get vell so I can get back on dat coal truck. One load of coal and my boy can't tell a vidow from a cheerleader. Erick, don't you go messin' around mitt Mary Vithers. Times is hard, and you'd be a catch for the likes of Mary Vithers."

The conversation quieted and remained that way for some time. It was Erick who seemed to dominate the sentimental banquet that the Muellers' simple dinner had become. He softly asked, "Mama, how long has it been since you heard from Otto?"

At the name of Otto, Hans struggled upward, slowly so as not to further agitate the spasm in his back. His face grimaced, whether from the pain of his back or hearing the word *Otto*, Erick wasn't sure. As his father lumbered back to the sofa, Erick repeated the significant part of his question. "How long?"

"Three years now, Erick. I sometimes wonder if he's even alive." Tears welled up in Ingrid's eyes. Erick felt badly that he had brought Otto up, yet it was as though it wasn't right not to.

Ingrid said nothing. Hans said nothing. Both Ingrid and Erick studied Hans. It was clear that something in his unforgiving and violent spirit had been tamed by the years. His previous frequent tirades against Otto had been muted by the passing of time. For many years Otto had been a forbidden subject of conversation. Now

Hans seemed to have forgotten that he had once had an ugly showdown with the boy. On the day that Otto left for the army, Hans had put forward a furious attempt to stop him. As Hans' anger grew, his accent became thicker. *"Otto,"* he had ordered, *"you must flee the draft. I vill send you to Australia on a ship. You must not go and fight with the Americans against our own volks."*

In spite of Hans' defiance, Otto had responded to the draft. Hans became so angry he had actually doubled his hand into a fist and hit Otto. The boy, bewildered by his father's anger, gave his parents a final look of hurt that had never left either of their minds.

It had been a terrible scene. Ingrid had cried and begged Hans not to hit Otto again. *"Please, Hans. You mustn't hit Otto."* Hans, still furious, had managed to curb his emotions but had shouted to his young son as he left the house, *"Never komm back. You are not velcome here, ever again."*

It was the last time any of them had seen Otto. They had received notice that he had suffered a major wound in France, and the resulting hospitalization had not only kept him from fighting in Germany but had left him with a distinct limp. Because of the injury, Otto never returned to active duty, so there was never any real accusation Hans could bring against his son for fighting against their relatives in Germany. Still, Hans had refused to lay aside his grudge because, as he had said, *"It vould be all der same if he had not been vounded. He vould have been right there firing on our own people."*

"Mama, I miss Otto. I would give anything to know what happened to him," whispered Erick, trying to hide his words from the old man, who had settled comfortably into the plump cushions of the couch. "Especially during the Christmas season, Mama. I always wonder how he's doing and where he is."

Ingrid reached out for Erick. His young arms were as thin as the rest of him, but they reached out for her and drew her up in an embrace. The strength of his arms closed her into love and understanding. Ingrid shuddered, chilled by old memories of that night long gone when the man she loved most had driven her firstborn, whom she loved much, out into a cold, torn world. In but a few moments of time, Hans had spent an open bit of vitriol, and for the past decade his words of anger had barred the gates of love against every hope that Otto might return.

But it wasn't Ingrid's tears that were most precious to Erick this night. As he held his weeping mother, his eyes fell upon the face of his father. And there he saw something he had never seen before. The strong round face was cut by streaks of penance. Never before had it happened. Yet it was happening now. Hans Mueller was weeping.

4

Two things happened on the night the old German coal man wept. First, arthritis, intuition, and public opinion once again joined forces, and the snow once more began to fall. Second, Alexis Withers developed a slight rattle in her chest that quickly developed into wheezing. Mary Withers shuddered. Alexis had barely made it through her last vicious attack in November. Now Mary faced the familiar enemy again. Upon the silent screen of her mind, there played the image of her child, whose torturous breathing could settle into a kind of stillness that did not even seem to be alive. She knew the demon of her child's asthma, for she had exorcised him often. The fiend was heartless; he would not even allow them a holiday. He would come as he always came. First the rattle in Alexis's chest would grow to a wheeze, and then the wheeze would deepen into violent gasping.

The gasping would at last try to strangle her little girl while she worked with Dr. Drummond to try to unpry the clammy fingers of the monster from her daughter's thin chest.

Mary walked, she did not run, to the phone. No panic in her steps. She never showed fear to either Alexis or to the foe. To be nervous was to concede. To be anxious a terrible mistake. What she would go through during the next few hours demanded that she pace her courage, rationing it out methodically, so there would be enough to last the night. She took the receiver out of the cradle, then held the cradle down and turned the hand crank.

The ringing of Dr. Drummond's phone on the other end could not muffle the eager clicks of a couple of neighbors who picked up their own receivers to listen in. The same line that serviced Mary's house served the Muellers' and several houses in between.

At last old Mrs. Samuels at central clicked on line. "Number please."

"Two-four-seven," Mary said.

"Certainly, Mary. I'll ring the doctor, but I can tell you he's been out at the Johnsons' most of the afternoon, trying to deliver a baby that's been slow in coming."

"Thank you, Mrs. Samuels." Mary's voice was urgent. She had no time to pick up Mrs. Samuels' invitation to gossip.

"Is it your little one again?" asked the operator. Nothing happened in the community that she didn't know all about. Mrs. Samuels seemed to view being a switchboard operator as a kind of profession. She was, after all, the source of the straight story for King of Prussia. Her facts were always right and always gathered by direct inquiry.

"Please, Mrs. Samuels. Will you ring Dr. Drummond?" Mary asked.

While waiting for Mrs. Samuels to make the connection, Mary's thoughts went to a recent conversation she'd had with Alexis.

"Mommy, do you miss Daddy?"

"What a thing to ask, Alexis. Of course I miss your father."

"I guess I do, too, but it seems like he's been gone so long I can hardly remember what he looked like."

Suddenly Alexis had coughed. Then she coughed again but with more violence than she had the first time.

"Alexis, you must not talk right now." Mary had gotten up and walked to the mantel and picked up a small frame. "Here's what your daddy looked like."

Alexis took the picture and studied it. "Mama, he has a mustache just like the coal man."

Mary blushed and turned away. Alexis had noticed something Mary as yet had not.

"Mama, the coal man brought us a lot of coal this

time—now we'll never get Caspian away from the fire."

Alexis stroked the big white cat and giggled, but her mirth ended abruptly in another cough and a long gasp for breath.

Mary then took the picture from Alexis and replaced it on the mantel.

"Mama, you talked to the coal man a long time, didn't you?"

"Alexis, why all this sudden interest in the coal man?"

"Well, Mama, you were laughing when you talked to him. I haven't seen you laugh out loud in a long time." Alexis then gasped so loudly it seemed to rattle deep down inside her.

"Alexis, please . . . no more talking."

Mary turned from her daughter's observation and concerned herself with Alexis's childish assessment. Was Alexis right? Had it been that long since Mary had laughed? She suddenly wondered what kind of grim guardian she had become. She despised the notion that she had become so serious about winning against the odds that the odds had cut all joy from her life.

The phone rang three times before it jangled Mary from her reverie. Then the receiver clicked. Mary breathed a sigh of relief as she heard a kind and familiar voice say, "The Drummonds'. Mrs. Drummond here."

"Marjie, it's Mary," said Mary matter-offactly. "Is Dr. Drummond there?"

"No, Mary, I'm so sorry. He's out at the Johnsons', trying to bring a little one into the world. Is everything all right? Is it Alexis?"

"Yes. Yes, it's Alexis. She's started one of her spells."

"Oh, I'm so sorry, Mary. I'll call the Johnsons and see how he's doing. I know he'll be there as soon as he can get there."

"Oh, thank you, Marjie. Thank you. Good-bye!"

"Good-bye, Mary. I'll be praying for you tonight, do you hear?"

"Yes, Marjie, good-bye!"

"Good-bye, Mary!"

Mary hung up the receiver. She turned toward Alexis's bedroom, squared her shoulders, and entered the child's room.

"Mommy," said Alexis, "will I be really sick again?"

"I can't say, Alexis. I'm praying it will not be as bad as it was the last time."

"Me too, Mommy. Every time I start feeling sick, I always ask God to never let it be as bad as it was the last time."

The phone rang. Mary jumped at the suddenness of its ring. She left Alexis, ran immediately into the next room, and grabbed the receiver off the hook. "Hello."

"Hello, Mary?"

"Yes, this is Mary. Marjie?"

"Yes. Mary, Dr. Drummond says the Johnsons have a fine little girl and he's on his way back to town. He also says the snow is getting heavier and he hopes it won't delay him from getting to you. He's going to send over some Ephedrine. Mary, you know what Dr. Drummond would say if he were there."

"Yes, Marjie, I know what he would say. He'd say, 'panic kills more people than the worst disease.'"

"Remember that, and keep a grip on things."

"I will, Marjie. Good-bye."

Mary returned to the room where Alexis was. She hated herself for not having the Ephedrine on hand. Still, money was always so close that she dared not spend it on medicine, speculating that Alexis might need it. After all, she had to pay bills to keep the present wolves at bay. Alexis's wheezing seemed a bit more constricting, but she was calmly reading a book.

"Where are your socks, girl!" Mary was frantic.

"The floor is warm, Mama," Alexis offered.

"There's a snow falling, child. You get your socks on."

Alexis fumbled in the bedclothes and extracted a pair of heavy wool anklets. "But the wool is so itchy!" she protested.

51

"Never you mind the itch; you keep your socks on!"

"But, Mama . . ."

Mary said nothing more, but the look she gave Alexis was enough to stop all conversation.

Mary settled into reading to Alexis. The book that Alexis preferred above all others was a Christmas story called *The Holly King*. In the hour that followed the wool socks rebuke, Mary read the volume through twice. She was in the process of putting on Alexis's pajamas when the phone rang. She hoped it would be Dr. Drummond. It was not.

"Hello."

"Hello, Mary. This is Janet Breckenridge. I just heard from one of your neighbors that Alexis is sick again."

Mary cringed at the speed of gossip in the town. The five-party telephone line knew no secrets. "Yes, Janet, Alexis is wheezing, but Dr. Drummond knows about it, and he will soon be home from the Johnsons'."

"Well, then, you haven't heard?"

"Heard what?

"Dr. Drummond's car slid off the road into the ditch three miles out of town. It's been snowing since midday in the country. The snow's getting so deep that Dr. Drummond decided to leave his car there till morning. The doctor himself is going to stay at Caslin's Dairy ... probably overnight."

Mary felt a clawing in the pit of her stomach. Alexis's strangling sickness had its fierce tentacles around her heart and wouldn't let go. Perhaps it was because Janet seemed so chipper in reporting the bad news that Mary felt herself growing angry. Like so many of the party-line gossips, Janet Breckenridge seemed to gloat in the telling of all news, good or bad. And Janet had to get the news first. This allowed her to be its primary keeper and afforded her the rare privilege of dumping it—usually with drama—on her ill-fated friends. Knowledge was power to Janet. She was a dowager collecting all kinds of news and then controlling her world by always being the first to inform it.

"Thanks for calling, Janet." Mary hung up. She was furious, but not too furious to begin counting. She knew that in the next sixty seconds the phone would ring again. This time it would be Mabel Cartwright, who, having just heard their conversation, would find it necessary to call. Even as she numbered the seconds on her trembling fingers, the phone rang. Mabel was right on time. Mary was tempted not to answer it, but on the possibility that it might be Dr. Drummond, she dared not let it ring too long.

She picked up the receiver and spoke hesitantly into the black celluloid mouthpiece. "Hello. Mary Withers."

"Mary, this is Mabel Cartwright. How are you, darling?"

"I'm fine, Mabel." Mary threw her the minimum number of syllables in order to kill a conversation she had no desire of prolonging.

"Mary, darling, I probably shouldn't say this, for of course it's no real business of mine, but I couldn't help noticing that for the past two nights your back chimney has been smoking. Now, Mary, I could have told you if you had asked—which of course you didn't—that running two stoves on opposite ends of the house is really not smart, even if you're doing it only at night. You may think it conceals your extravagance to burn the extra coal at night when nobody can see the smoke. But I saw it pale against the clouds, Mary. Be sure your sins will find you out. In fact, Mary dear, I wonder if it's really prudent for you to try that on your meager income. There's no use heating all of your house while you are still ordering your coal by the eighth of a ton—at least that's what Hans told my Henry in the barbershop. Of course I am thinking more about Alexis than about your unfortunate economy. But let me go on, Mary. As I say, if you had asked me I might have told you that running that back chimney was going to create a draft through your entire house. It's the very kind of irregular ventilation that asthmatics do not need!"

Mary was exasperated! She bit her lower lip and remembered how the good Lord had counseled all people to love their enemies, though she couldn't help but wonder if Jesus really understood Mabel Cartwright. But then it *was* Christmas Eve, so after counting to ten backwards, Mary managed enough charity to say, "Thank you, Mabel. Have a good night!" Mary cradled the receiver very abruptly and added, "And don't let the bed bugs bite, or maybe they should bite. Likely they'd spit it out if they did!"

Once her anger subsided, Mary Withers could tell that Alexis was breathing more roughly with each passing minute. She walked to the window and tried to see out, but the snow was now falling so thickly there was no possibility of seeing anything. Mary tucked Alexis in bed, then walked back to the great room and stoked the fire in the potbellied stove. She watched as the hypnotic flames ate the new black lumps, then danced around the blue edges of those embers that were once as black as those they devoured.

The stove's firebox seemed a parable of Mary's life. Her one fiery hope was that Alexis would survive childhood. This eternal flame at the center of her life would never go out as long as she had the slightest reason to hope. But around that fiery center was a kind of fearsome deadness that isolated her from the world. *"Ashes must always be blown away from the outside if ever you keep the fire in the center,"* her Amish grandmother had often told her. How much Mary had come to characterize the proverb. While Mary mused on the saying, she heard Alexis's wheezing slowing and returned to her side. Alexis watched her mother with wistful eyes that seemed to have something so worth saying that it could not wait until the asthma had passed.

"Mama," said Alexis, "was it cold in the stable the night the two wise men came?"

"I don't know," answered Mary. "Maybe. Whatever made you ask such a question?"

"Well, I just wondered if baby Jesus ever got sick, that's all."

"I'm sure he must have from time to time."

"Know what I like about baby Jesus?"

"No, I don't, Alexis. What do you like?"

"Well, Mama, both of us have a mother named Mary."

Mary was dumbfounded by the child's thoughtful statement.

"Mama, what was Jesus' mother's last name?"

The question, which seemed so logical to Alexis, seemed almost comical to Mary. The truth was she had no idea. "Well, Alexis, I don't know that I ever heard her last name. People have always just called her Mary of Nazareth, because that's where she was from. Back then, you just called people by the name of the place where they lived."

"Then if Jesus' mother was called Mary of Nazareth, could you be called Mary of King of Prussia?"

The child's sincerity caused Mary to burst into laughter. Then seeing Alexis's apparently serious demeanor, Mary got hold of herself. "I suppose," she replied, "but it would seem kind of odd in our day and age." Mary had been into many odd conversations with her inquisitive daughter, but she could not immediately see where, if anywhere, this conversation was headed.

"Well, Mama, Christmas got started when Jesus was born, didn't it?"

"Indeed, Alexis."

"Do you remember what Reverend Schultz said last week in the sermon?"

"Not everything, Alexis. *What in particular?*"

"He said that we are all the children of God. Did he mean big people too? He said that even Mary and Joseph were the children of God. That must mean that God loved Mary because she was his little girl just like Mary loved Jesus 'cause he was her little boy. Is that right?"

Sometimes Alexis's conversation forced

Mary to grapple with both her childlike innocence and the incredible wisdom that children often possess.

"Yes, I think so," said Mary. It seemed too simple, but Alexis had the entire idea of Christmas figured out pretty well.

"Did Reverend Schultz mean you and me and the coal man? Did he mean that all of us are the children of God?"

"Yes. Yes, he did." Mary couldn't understand why once again Alexis was including the coal man in their conversation.

"Well then, that must mean that God loves you just like you love me."

"I guess so."

"So, Mama, if I were God and I loved you like you love me, I would want you to have the happiest Christmas ever. And you know what, Mama? I wouldn't let your little girl have a serious asthma attack on Christmas Day."

Mary turned her face away to hide her tears. Things were so simple for Alexis.

Alexis quit talking. In spite of her bright philosophy, her wheezing was now coming so thickly that it was keeping her from talking very loud or for very long.

"Alexis, Mama doesn't want you to talk anymore right now."

"Okay, Mama," Alexis said. Her short agreement came between shuddering gasps. Spasms arched her little back and threw her tiny chest upward, enabling her to inhale enough air to make life possible. To anyone unfamiliar with asthma, it would appear that the disease could get no worse. But Mary knew better.

Outside in the dark, the heavy white blanket of snow fell like a felted hammer, but ever so quietly. The house creaked under the silent weight the storm was imposing upon it. Mary knew that Dr. Drummond would not be coming. Whatever the night brought, she would face it alone. "Do not be afraid, Mary," she whispered to herself. But she was unconvincing. Alexis began to cough violently, and fear crouched darkly in the shadowed corners of Mary's mind.

"God," breathed Mary, "give me the childlike faith of Alexis. I need something to help me. Give me some sign, please . . . please! It's Christmas, God. I don't want anything grand. I just want Alexis to live. Please . . . just that. I need to know."

Alexis's cough began to calm—her spasms came less incessantly. At last Mary felt free to cry and took a long deserved turn at weeping. Thinking she was unobserved, Mary was surprised to feel the warm hand of little Alexis reach over the side of the bed and lay itself on Mary's arm. "Mama," she said sleepily, "don't cry. God comes as quietly as the snow. He's all around us, isn't He, Mama? And you'll see, Mama, I'm going to be all right. We are all the children of God."

It sounded simple, yet oddly mature.

"Thank you, Alexis," said Mary. "Now, darling, you must get some rest."

Alexis said nothing but crooked her tiny index finger, beckoning her mother to bring her face close to her own. Then when Mary was quite close, Alexis's little arm flew instantly up and pulled Mary's head very close, and Alexis kissed her mother on the forehead.

It was sign enough. The kiss lingered, cool and wet, and Mary knew that though the kiss had come from Alexis, it was sent from somewhere else. *It is innocence*, thought Mary, *that allows the God of Christmas to speak his hope through sick children.* With the kiss it seemed she heard from heaven itself—a whispered voice in the gales beyond the frosted windowpanes. Yes. Yes. She was sure now. She was not at all sure Alexis was going to be all right, but she was sure God would be with them both no matter what happened. The heart will hear what it needs to when its longings are severe. She knew that the Almighty had not forgotten her, and He had wrapped every promise of his presence in a child's kiss. But this was the best part: A promise followed the kiss. Mary was sure that she heard the night whisper, "We are all the children of God."

The fire crackled.

Wind threw handfuls of snow against the windowpanes.

And Mary of King of Prussia smiled into the amber darkness. Whatever happened, she was not alone.

Erick listened to his mother cracking walnuts in the next room. He loved the sounds of Christmas. They always came first, just before the smells of Christmas. On Christmas Eve Ingrid always cracked walnuts. Hans had splurged and bought one of the seven turkeys the Johnsons had raised that year. Turkeys were scarce even during the opening days of the depression, and the Johnsons, insisting that Hans sometimes shorted them on coal, decided to charge the coal man more for the bird than they might have if he had been a little more generous with them back in earlier winters. Hans paid the Johnsons but refused to "vish them a merry Christmas." Having made a mental note of their high-priced turkey, he vowed to get even with them during the February deliveries. He would get back the entire overcharge by March. Coal was the way in which he both blessed and settled all grudges with his world.

In the meantime, Ingrid had her turkey. Hans had killed it that morning, and it was hanging on the screened-in porch, ready to face a hot Christmas oven.

In the morning the aromas of mincemeat—along with the extra walnuts they all liked—would be mingling with the smell of roasting turkey. The giblet broth would complete the trio of odors that for the past twenty-five years had brought Erick scrambling from his bed on Christmas morning. *Come snow*, Erick thought to himself. *Bury us, if you can.*

The night was young but cold, and the snow so deep that Erick rejoiced there was not one earthly reason he would have to get out in the cold. Somewhere near eight o'clock the phone rang. "I'll get it, Mama!" he shouted, jumping up from the chair and out of his reverie. In but two of his lanky steps he was at the phone. He took the pear-shaped receiver off its little chrome hook.

"Hello! This is the Muellers'!"

"Hans, is that you?" asked the faraway voice on the other end of the line.

"No, it's Erick!"

"Erick?"

"Yes!"

"Erick, this is Dr. Drummond. Nice to have you home from the university."

"Thanks. It's great to be home!"

"Erick, is your truck working?"

"Yes, of course, so far, but the snow is piling up."

"Erick, I'm trapped out at Caslin's Dairy, and I can't get home. I hate to ask this of you, but could you possibly go by the clinic? Marjie will meet you there and give you a parcel of medicine for the Withers baby. I know it's a bad night, but would you mind?"

Erick could hardly believe his good fortune. Mary Withers! It must be Christmas, Christmas indeed! He had not managed to free his mind of her laughter since his morning delivery. And her face? Just the memory of her face said "Merry Christmas." Suddenly Erick lost the world at hand. He was back in the gray morning delivering coal. He was down on his knees, groveling on the cold threshold of the Witherses' house, grappling for a coal bin key. Suddenly two eyes were gazing at him through the fog on his spectacles—the eyes of a woman who, for reasons he could not fathom, would not go away. He saw her framed in the doorway like Isis in gingham . . . like . . .

"Erick, are you still there?" asked Dr. Drummond.

"He's still there," said Mabel Cartwright butting in from her extension. "Erick, talk to

Dr. Drummond. Will you take the medicine or not?"

"Mabel, this is not your affair. Get off the line."

Mabel never hung up, but Erick did return to the conversation that his reverie had interrupted. "I'd love to, Dr. Drummond . . . that is, if I can get the truck moving through the snow. It should work. I don't think the snow is all that deep yet here in town."

"Erick, I don't know how to thank you. I wouldn't ask, but it really could be a matter of life and death."

"Not to worry. Say no more, Dr. Drummond."

"Tell Hans I'll order an extra ton of coal in January."

"Please, Dr. Drummond. You owe us nothing. I'm glad to help out. I guarantee you Hans won't mind, and forget about ordering extra coal. It's as good as done! Good-bye."

"Thanks again. Good-bye!"

Erick hung up as soon as Dr. Drummond did.

"Vhat is this? Vhat von't I mind, Erick?"

"I told Dr. Drummond you wouldn't mind if I used the truck to take some medicine out to the Witherses."

"And vhy did you tell him he didn't have to order extra coal when you know perfectly vell it's how ve make our living?"

"It's Christmas, Papa. Charity should own the season."

"I'll tell you vhat owns the season—it's thrift. I'll tell you vhat is the best Christmas present of all—it's freedom from debt. So far you haven't given the voman anything except a half ton of my coal. Be sure you don't give her anything else. Ingrid! Come in here and tell your demented son to leave that Vithers vidow alone. He listens to you. Ingrid! Come talk to the boy!"

"You talk. I agree with the boy. Mary Withers is a saint in need of a little help. There isn't a soul in town who doesn't admire her as a person who is taking the lemons of life and turning them into lemonade. She wrestles every day with hardship. Hans, maybe on Christmas Eve we could all let up a little."

The sound of walnut chopping stopped for a moment and then started again. Ingrid never left the kitchen, preferring not to arbitrate the rift that was developing between the two favorite men in her life.

"Ingrid! Ingrid!" Hans called louder.

Ingrid started chopping walnuts again, louder than before. The big knife was coming down hard on the chopping block, giving Hans his answer. "Handle this yourself, Hans. I've got walnuts to chop."

"Well, Papa, I'm gonna run this medicine out

to the Witherses. Maybe we can do a little something for our neighbors this Christmas Eve."

"You come right back. Don't try to spend the evening mitt der black vidow of King of Prussia. Do you hear me, Erick? If you are feeling romantic, you can just vait till you're back at Syracuse to do your courtin'."

"Yes, Papa!" said Erick, pulling on his high-top boots. He tried not to look in his father's direction as he belted his woolen jacket around his middle. He doubled his felt scarf around his neck and then pulled on his red wool cap. He secured the earflaps over his ears by tying under his chin the thin cord that dangled from the end of each flap like a knotted shoelace.

At last Ingrid put in an appearance, acting as though she had no idea what was happening. "Where on earth are you going in this storm, Erick?" she asked, coming in from the kitchen.

"I'll tell you vhere he's going, Ingrid. He's going to der Vitherses'. He says it's because Dr. Drummond asked him to. But I've never seen the lad move so fast in my life. I think he's got a case for that Vithers vidow!"

"Now, Erick, tie your earflaps," Ingrid ordered, kissing him on the cheek even as she turned her back on Hans.

"I already have, Mama!" said Erick, pausing with his hand on the doorknob, ready to rush out into the weather.

"Erick, don't you get yourself stuck out there overnight. You know how Mabel Cartwright loves a good story."

"I won't, Mother!" Erick insisted.

"I von't, mother!" mocked Hans. "I tell you, Ingrid, you better tie the boy's earflaps to your apron strings if you vant him back by the New Year."

"Papa, be quiet. Mama, go chop your walnuts. I'm a grown man with a mind of my own."

He dashed out, slamming the door just as Hans murmured, "Some mind he's got. He ought to use it more than he does. Anyvay he von't go far vithout these." Hans drew a bulky key ring from his pocket.

They were barely out of his pocket when the hastily slammed door flew open and Erick reappeared in a swirl of wind and snow. "Papa..."

"You vere looking for these." Hans dangled the truck keys in front of the lad.

Erick grabbed them, but Hans held on. "Promise me you von't get thick mitt the Vithers vidow."

Erick pulled hard and with a suddenness that jerked the keys from his father's fat hand. "No promises. Merry Christmas, Papa!"

He leapt out once more into the wind-driven snow.

"Ingrid, the boy is hopeless! I think I'd disown him if he'd stand still longer."

"Hans," said Ingrid, "let up on the boy. It's Christmas!"

"Some excuse for stealing a man's truck and giving avay his coal."

"It's the snow, Hans! It brings the most unlikely sorts of people together. You know what they say, 'December love and snow both melt after Christmas.' "

Erick used an old broom and brushed the snow off the windshield of the truck. Then he leapt inside and thrust the key into the ignition. The motor roared to life. He backed out of the driveway and turned the truck in the direction of Dr. Drummond's house.

First he would get the medicine, then he would head toward the Witherses' house. It was not just Christmas, it was somehow a nativity of the spirit. Then he chided his overpoetic notion. *That was just the kind of corny idea a mathematician might have*, he thought. But Erick wasn't just any old mathematician. He was in love. He wondered if Mary Withers was also in love. He dared to hope that fumbling with the simple key to her coal bin had somehow unlocked something inside them both.

"God, what am I to do?" Mary breathed. It was both a prayer to God and a question to herself. She made herself a cup of tea and for the next thirty minutes thought of all that had happened that day. But of all the events, it was the mercy of the generous young coal vendor that most occupied her mind. She so much enjoyed keeping Erick at the center of her reverie. But suddenly her thoughts of Erick ended with a gasp. Two words that she had stored at the back of her mind in the afternoon suddenly moved forward—*back chimney!* What did Mabel Cartwright mean by the odd idea? The entire back of the house was sealed, precisely so she wouldn't have to heat it. Could Mabel have been mistaken? She must have been. The very idea that the back chimney was smoking made her flesh crawl. Could there be someone living in the back of her house? No, it wasn't possible. She left Alexis's bedroom, and when she was far enough away from Alexis that the child's gasping would not interrupt her, she listened intently with her ear to the door in the center wall that led to the back section of the house. Nothing. She heard nothing and was comforted.

Whether it was the power of suggestion or not, just after eight o'clock Mary experienced the grip often unknown. She thought—no, she was *certain*—she heard a loud knocking coming from the dark part of her house, after all. She might have determined to seek the source of the strange and unwelcome noise except for one thing: fear.

Mary Withers was suddenly afraid, of what she didn't know. *I know everything about the back part of my house.* At the center of its four rooms was a small sitting room and an old kitchen. The entire area was warmed by a woodburning range that provided enough heat to warm the sitting room, the kitchen, and a small fourth bedroom. Two of her grandmother's needle-point pictures hung in the rear kitchen. One said *Prayer Changes Things*, and the other read *Go to the Ant, Thou Sluggard, and be Wise*. A door led to a staircase that went down to the east end of the long basement. In the center of the hallway, a stone partition with a door separated the east and west halves of the basement. What was there not to know about the sealed part of her house?

It was Christmas Eve and a time for extending good will to all, yet she eyed the poker leaning against the wall behind the glowing stove. She had no idea how to use a poker as a weapon, but she fancied the iron thing as a kind of stubby Excalibur, waiting to serve her. *Fear fashions courage into weapons*, she thought. In better light, in happier conversations, she would have smiled at the notion of sallying out to do battle with a poker. But now she was genuinely afraid.

She struggled with the huge buffet that flanked the east wall of her room and managed to shove it against the door that connected the friendly front part of her house to the dark and haunted rooms at the rear. Then the prickles of fear began to grow. In the next quarter of an hour, her mind changed the silence in her home to disturbing sounds. She thought she heard sandpapery, ominous footfalls somewhere down below and a strange clanking, like coal dropping into a tin scuttle. It was those basement noises, whether real or otherwise, that terrified her. Staring at the door now barricaded by the bureau, she suddenly remembered that it was not the only way into the other part of her home. There was also that door in the basement, just beyond the coal bin.

The basement door!

She shuddered at the thought of it and looked at the floor, as though looking at it would help her hear a little better any noise beneath it. Was something or someone down there?

No. Nothing.

She rebuked her fears. But her fears turned on her and argued back. Should she go down and inspect it? She didn't want to for one very important reason. The house had come late to be electrified, and to save money, the previous owners had not put electricity in the basement. So whatever tour of inspection she had planned, she would have to carry it off with a lantern or candle. But the lantern was in the basement, so she would have to use a candle to locate it. Something had to be done, and she was the only one who could do it.

So Mary Withers did the most courageous thing she had done in years. She picked up her stubby Excalibur, lit a candle, and went to the basement to battle the foe she was unwilling to imagine. Her own footfalls on the creaking stairs sounded eerie. The candle shadows fell ahead of her like dark felting on a planked staircase. Not until she reached the basement did she feel the welcome joy of breathing again.

How foolish she had been. The candle flame told all, and the telling was a glorious mercy in the dank darkness of the basement.

There was no one there. Nor to all appearances had there been. Still, she would make assurance double sure. Since the basement door to the other part of the house was unbolted, she would make it secure. She had never before felt a need to bolt it. But this was somehow a fearsome Christmas Eve. She took the old steel bolt from the lintel and slipped it through the hasp, securing the basement entrance to the rear of the house. It occurred to her that she ought to go on through the basement door and complete her exploration of the empty eastern rooms of her house, but she did not.

"Mama! Where are you?" She could hear her daughter call to her from the upper part of the house.

Alexis, she thought, *how wonderful to hear your voice.* The child's tiny call held the kind of music that erases specters.

"Mama!" cried Alexis again. Even from the basement, Mary could tell Alexis was in trouble.

"God," Mary begged as she climbed the stairs, "tonight I need you. Help me!"

Mabel Cartwright's odd counsel faded. There was no one in the dark part of her house. Mabel must have been mistaken. Mabel was, however, the perfect person to announce the witches of Christmas Eve. Who would know a witch better than Mabel? Then Mary Withers felt ashamed. She had no right to be snide, even within her heart. She had a daughter who could bless the world with charity. She resolved to try to get enough innocence in her own life to wish even Mabel Cartwright the best of the season.

No more noise came from the sealed-off part of the house.

Mary sat down again by Alexis's bed and wished she could do something more than merely sit. But sitting has its place, and to wait is oftentimes to serve. God seemed all about her, and the fears moved back; the noises ceased. Earlier the silence had seemed eerie. Now it seemed to be filled with the same odd presence Mary had felt earlier. Only Alexis's struggle for breath broke the quiet.

There would be no services at the church this Christmas Eve. The snow had put an end to a most important event of this Pennsylvania Christmas.

The same snow that isolated Mary with her needy Alexis performed a kind of visual wonder in town. The streetlight, softly flooding the Muellers' snow-crowned mailbox, gave notice to Ingrid that the red flag was still up. She had raised it earlier to mail a few last-minute Christmas cards. The flag struck at her with the realization that she had not gone to the mailbox that day.

"Hans," said Ingrid, "I forgot to get the mail."

"Probably nothing came. It's Christmas Eve!"

"Still, I'd better check . . . could be something there."

"Vell, then, bundle up vhen you go out."

Ingrid did not need the counsel, but she acted on it. Though Hans' galoshes were huge, she decided to wear them since it was only a short trip. She pulled on her gloves, then wrapped a scarf around her head twice so that only her eyes were showing. Finally, she donned Hans' old mackinaw and opened the door. The snow whirled inward, hissing at the warmth inside the house. Pulling the door closed behind her, she reveled in the white world about her and felt that odd sensation of vertigo that snow imparts when it refuses to fall downward. To be sure most of it falls downward, but some of it appears to rise upward. Then, in perfect defiance of gravity and all sense, some of it never falls at all. It just goes around and around in midair.

Ingrid studied Hans through the huge front window. The tree beside him begged for candle fire. It would look beautiful from the outside, only the weather was so bad there would be no passersby to see it when they lit the candles. Perhaps even prettier than the tree inside were the two large pines in the front yard which were already dressed for the hallowed evening. Snow in the streetlights created Magic. The evening itself was Magic, and she knew that even Hans would believe it Magic since all his customers would be burning lots of coal.

Ingrid stopped her wonderment and crunched her way down the unshoveled walk to the picket gate and out into the empty street, where she turned abruptly toward her house and faced the mailbox. She put the postman's flag down, and then reached in under the canopy of snow and pulled out a single letter. It was a small square envelope that wouldn't lie flat for the bulky burden of something it contained. Ingrid shook the envelope, and it rattled. This curious survey found her staring for several seconds at the envelope with her arms extended. Snowflakes passed between her eyes and the letter. It was not for her. Even in the scant streetlight, she could tell it was addressed to Hans. Somewhat disappointed, she made a new set of footprints going in the opposite direction of those she had just scrubbed into the snow. Gratefully she stepped back into her doorway and closed the weather out with a sigh. "Whew! Hans, people ought to use a lot of coal tonight!"

"*Das is gut! Gut! Gut!* Vhen they all get cold, ve vill all get rich—maybe!" replied Hans, rising on one elbow from his couch with a twinkle in his eye.

After Ingrid had taken off the mackinaw and hung it back on the shaker-peg coatrack just inside the door, Hans set aside the paper he'd been reading and watched her as she studied the odd, square envelope she had brought in from the mailbox. Ingrid liked the idea of heightening the drama, even in the most minor of mysteries. Out of the corner of her eyes, she could tell that she had the complete attention of her none-too-patient husband. So she forced a deliberate slowness into her step as she crossed the room, poured herself a cup of coffee, and retraced her steps to her favorite Chippendale chair across the room from Hans. She settled down with a stage sigh and crossed her legs. Once again she studied the odd envelope, took a long, relaxed sip of coffee, and set her cup down.

"For goodness' sake, Ingrid, open it!" said Hans, who was more than a little vexed by the enormous amount of time she was taking.

"Hold your horses, you old Bavarian!" she sniped. "It's addressed to you. Will it be okay if I open it?"

"Do I have anything to hide? Open it, Ingrid, open it." Hans was most impatient, and his agitated need to have her hurry only increased her desire to be more deliberate.

So, dutifully and ever so slowly, she picked up a paper slitter from the drum table and opened the mysterious envelope. A long thin silver chain fell out.

No small shiny bit of metal could have fallen with more force on the heart of the old man. He knew the chain. It ended with a silver cross, still as shiny as the day he had given it to their exiled son some twelve years earlier. He well remembered the day of Otto's confirmation when he had made him a present of the very chain Ingrid now wound around her fingers. The pain in his lower back could not prevent his reaching out toward Ingrid to wrest the chain from her hand. She drew back, clutching the chain in the same hand she now used to draw a piece of paper from the envelope. Hans continued reaching out as if to take the letter and the chain. Ingrid stood, finally managing to evade his pursuit.

Hans could only watch her as she read. Never had he beheld her face so knotted with intention. When she had read for fully five minutes, she bit her bottom lip, almost till it bled. Then she turned away from Hans, her small frame convulsing. She remained with her back turned till she was fully in control again. She kept the chain but handed the letter to her husband.

Hans took it and began to read.

Dear Papa and Mama:

There are so many things I am sorry for. But the one act I most regret is that which occurred on that awful July day in 1917 when I turned away from you and honored my draft board commitments. I now weep that, by obeying the law, I severed forever my chance to return home. Until Black Tuesday, I had my own apartment in Man-

hattan and was doing financially very well. But my hope and my fortune crashed on Wall Street. I lost everything and all at once. But never could I lose as much as I lost the day I dishonored your wishes.

I have turned over and over in my mind the size of my offense in refusing to take the money you offered me to flee to Australia and avoid the draft. I know you were informed that I was wounded early in the conflict and that I never got to help with the battle of Amiens. So, Papa, I never had to wage war against any of our family. I hoped this might make it easier for you to forgive me for the hurt I have caused you.

I have no money, and I have been unable to find any work. It is cold this winter, and I am not sure I can survive much longer on the streets. If you never hear from me again, please know that I will forever lament the hurt I caused you, and I will go to my grave grieving our estrangement. I will always love the three of you. I pray for all of you every night of my life. I pray that God will supply you the greatest Christmas you have ever known. Knowing you can never esteem me, I return this chain you gave me on the day of my confirmation. It reminds me too much of the disappointment I have brought you.

Your son, who never deserved to wear so grand a word . . . Otto

For a long time after Hans quit reading, he stared straight ahead. "Ingrid," he said at last,

Eagerly Hans tore the envelope from her grasp.

He, too, studied the envelope!

"Ingrid! Ingrid! Can it be? Can Otto be so near? Call the constable! Ve must find him."

The letter that had brought the immigrant couple such heavy introspection was eclipsed by a circular smudge of ink, stamped *King of Prussia, Pennsylvania*. Because of this small circlet of postal ink, Hans instantly believed all the impossible things of Christmas. Snow was making Pennsylvania into a land of wonder, a land of God's best gifts. Hans believed in Christmas, he believed in angels singing over ancient hillsides, the star, the wise men, the virgin and all the miracles born in the soft crush of new snow.

2

By nine-thirty Alexis's condition had become critical, and Mary was desperate for the Ephedrine. She knew she must have it, yet had no idea how she was going to get it through the horrendous storm. She did not panic, but tears of fear camped in her eyes. In this moment of utter despair, her desperation received an answer. A loud knocking came from the front door of the house. *In this storm? Someone at my door? It must be that wonderful old doctor who makes Christmas come to widows and children*, she thought. She leapt from the couch like a coiled spring and scurried to the door. But even before she could get there, the hurried banging came once again. She knew the knock. It was Dr. Drummond. "Thank you, God, for such a wonderful physician," she said aloud as she reached for the inside knob.

"Dr. Drummond!" she cried, throwing the door open.

"Sorry, Mrs. Withers, it's the coal man," said Erick Mueller with a smile.

"What?"

"Dr. Drummond sent me to his dispensary. You've heard he's going to be holed up at least till morning at Caslin's Dairy? He asked me to bring you the Ephedrine and said you'd know what to do with it."

"W-won't you come in?"

It was an uncertain invitation, and Erick might not have responded to it had the weather been better. After he had done his best to brush the snow off his mackinaw outside the door, he entered the room. He handed the small parcel of medicine to Mary. She took it. Once more in the awkward moment of exchange, their eyes met. Each instantly turned away.

"Mary, could I use your phone?"

"Yes, of course, Erick. But don't say anything you wouldn't want instantly known and reported. We have no secrets out this way. Take off your coat, and I'll make some coffee."

While Mary hurried off to the kitchen, she heard Erick saying, "No, Mama, I'm all right. Won't soon get the truck back on the road, though. I'll warm up here before I start home. It'll be a long walk, but . . . No, Mama, I can't stay here. I'm at Mary Withers' place. You know Janet Breckenridge will have it all over town in the morning."

"Well, I never . . ." interjected Janet from her receiver.

"Janet, hang up! This is none of your business."

Erick heard Janet's receiver click. He felt relieved, but not for long. "Mabel, are you listening too?"

She was, and hung up before he had a chance to rebuke her.

"Anyway, Mama, I'll start home after I have myself a warm . . . How much snow have we had, Mama? Do you know? Tell Papa I got the truck stuck. It won't be hard to dig out, but I got away without the scoop. It must be over twelve inches now, and it's drifting a bit. It just keeps coming. . . . Yes, Mama, I'll be careful. . . . Yes, I'll bundle up too. . . . Mama, I'd better hang up now."

"No, not yet, Erick."

For Erick, the party-line roaches were an annoyance. But for Ingrid Mueller, they were a threat against the burgeoning secret that was now so large with joy it seemed her happiness would burst. Still, she would have to wait to tell Erick about Otto's letter and the local postmark lest a party-line indiscretion should destroy her great news in a blitz of gossip. "Erick, I have something to tell you when you get home."

"What's that, Mama?"

"It's something God has given the Muellers for Christmas."

"Well then, what, Mama?"

"Just you wait, son." Again she repeated, "You just be careful in this storm. Merry Christmas, Erick!"

"Merry Christmas, Mama. Good-bye."

Mary reentered the room. "I couldn't help overhearing your conversation with your mother." Then, trying to mask her too earnest concern, she added more casually, "Please, Erick, don't try to walk anywhere in this weather. And thanks so much for bringing the medicine for Alexis."

"Have you given it to her yet?"

"I just did! Sometimes the medicine works fast, and she gets better instantly. Let us hope this is one of those times. If her breathing gets easier, I hold back on the Ephedrine. Don't you leave, Erick Mueller. I'll be back in two shakes with the hottest coffee on the east side of King of Prussia."

Mary laughed. So did Erick. Mary could not know how much Erick enjoyed hearing her laugh. And Erick didn't realize that it was the first time in several hours that Mary had done so. Mary felt both guilty and healed for that brief moment. She felt good and then guilty and then good again for not remaining preoccupied with Alexis.

True to her word, Mary was back in the two shakes she had promised. She placed a small tray with a fine china cup and a tall china pot on the small table beside his chair. It was her finest china, and she rarely used it for fear that using it would shorten its life. But in Mary's mind the occasion merited the risk. She had a new friend who had found her in the rippling bright cold and the vaulting flurries of silver flakes.

"They seem to feel around town that you're a person of great strength," offered Erick awkwardly.

Mary Withers was not used to compliments. She reddened and then stammered out a reply as awkward as the compliment. "Why? Why would anyone say such a thing?"

"Well, Mary Withers, it seems that most everyone around here admires—"

" . . . a widow with a sick child."

"Yes, but it's more than that."

"What do you mean?"

"I think you're a woman who copes and wins. You struggle, I'm sure, but, Mary, you survive. Life hasn't been very kind to you, yet you show kindness to everyone you meet."

Mary fidgeted. Whatever Erick might have had in mind with his compliments, the words made Mary uncomfortable, and she tried to change the subject. "Erick, tell me about life at the university."

"I doubt if it's as interesting as your own life."

"Please stop all this complimentary stuff and tell me about life at the university."

"Well, I teach. I'm a good teacher too—if I do say so. Mary, there's an excitement in standing before a group of students and opening up to them new ways of looking at the world. But it's more than that. Sometimes I get a student who really doesn't believe in herself. And it's a wonderful thing to show her that she's unique and sent by the good Lord to change her part of the world. I like students. I want to help them root out their insecurities and give them more than a lecture. I want to furnish them with something positive and courageous that will put a little starch in their backbones and give them the power to order doubt out of their lives and careers."

Mary listened but couldn't help glancing in the direction of Alexis.

Erick noticed, and his philosophizing suddenly seemed insensitive even to him.

"Forgive me, Mary—I mean, Mrs. Withers."

"I'm sorry, Erick." Mary was on the verge of tears, then she got hold of herself. "Please don't call me Mrs. Withers, Professor Mueller." At the very formal term, Erick laughed abruptly, inelegantly spewing a bit of coffee across his chin. His sputtering laughter caused Mary to smile as she handed him a napkin, but she didn't laugh. The heavy world was crushing her under its weight.

Erick felt ashamed for being so lighthearted when she was underneath the burden of this cold, demanding Christmas Eve.

"Mary, please don't think me forward," he said quietly, "but there are a million things I should like to learn from you. You seem to live here so comfortably. I want you to teach me how to see this small town. I want to learn how to walk among these people we both know so well and not resent them for their provincial notions. I want to learn to see the world with a vision made clear by the sting of cold air. I need to know how to deal with life, harsh as it sometimes is."

"Whoa, there! You can't suppose I know all those things? No, Erick, I don't know them. They are lessons I need as badly as you feel you need them. I hate to take the sheen from my reputation, but, Erick, I'm frightened sometimes, and I'm very frightened tonight. It took all I had to survive after Tom's death. I thought I would never quit being afraid at night. And all the strength I appear to have is a kind of bravado I put on so that Alexis will find a chance at happiness. Yet the winters here are always cold, and the snow around Tom's gravestone puts a chill on the future. And there's Alexis. The doctor has been frank. If I can keep Alexis alive till she's nine or ten, then . . ."

Mary stopped and bit her lower lip. She didn't cry, but the clear pain that filled her eyes fashioned itself into drops that nearly spilled over her cheeks before she blotted the corner of her eyes.

She stood to turn away. Erick stood, too, and instinctively reached for her. She maintained her distance, but Erick didn't. In a moment he was at her side, then gently he turned her toward himself and held her close.

Sensing Erick's tender concern, Mary could no longer keep up her pretense of courage, and she began to sob. Erick held her fragile, needy form and discovered in that moment that he loved Mary furiously. The dustman reached out his hands to accept the fetters of a strange new emotion.

He wanted to kiss her. He cupped her chin and turned her wet face upward toward his own.

"No, please don't," she whispered, lowering her eyes with embarrassment.

"Mary, I won't. Never without your permission. But all that I am now feeling cannot wait for anyone's approval."

Mary wriggled from his more relaxed embrace and said, "Erick, you have brought laughter back into this house and made this sickroom a place of warmth and joy. When you were talking, I realized how very lonely I have been. Alexis's illness has consumed my life. Oh, how grateful I am for this snow, for it has washed me in Christmas. I thought that jargon about love and good cheer was dull and unrealistic, but for all my insecurity there's Magic in this snow. No, more than Magic—healing, perhaps. Erick, my grief has been my bread and drink far too long. It wasn't just Tom I buried in the winter of '26. In a sense I climbed into Tom's grave that day, only here and there digging my soul out for the sake of poor Alexis. If I am a woman capable of love, I never unearthed myself till this morning. I cannot afford to repeat this risky business until both of us are sure. Do you understand?"

"Yes, Mary, I do."

"Then let us speak no more of all of this till there is some more level occasion, if such a time can be."

"But the time is not out there *somewhere*, Mary. The time is now. And do not think you are the only one eager to walk away from the grave. I have a brother somewhere in the world, whether dead or alive, I'm not sure. He served in the army, much against my father's wishes. As a result of all this, for years there has been an estrangement at the center of our family. This morning I caught my mother crying. It happens every Christmas Eve. And never does the crying begin without it bringing to mind the awful scene twelve years ago when my father struck my brother, Otto, and ordered him out of our home forever. Otto has haunted our every Christmas since. My father sees his ghost on the surface of the wassail that Otto so loved, and my mother longs to see him once again. And to be truthful, his leaving took something from my life that only his return could ever restore. We were so close growing up that I think I shall never be complete again. If only I could know for sure Otto is dead, then I could grieve and get past him. But the not knowing has left my whole family chained to a specter that haunts us year by year."

Mary listened as carefully as she could.

In his talking and her listening their faces were magnetically drawn together. Again Mary realized their conversation was pushing their relationship too rapidly. She stiffened herself, sitting more upright. Erick followed suit, and the intimacy of their double confession turned suddenly more businesslike.

"Tell me, Erick," Mary said, completely changing the subject, "why have you never married? You must be King of Prussia's most eligible bachelor. You must be over—" Mary realized she was about to shatter all things conventional. She actually blushed a little at the forwardness of her near blunder.

"Yes, Mary, no need to worry about propriety. I am over twenty-seven. Unlike my brother, I was just young enough to miss the draft. After the war I received a referral from the draft board so that I could stay home and help with the family business. I don't feel like an eligible bachelor. Every year I teach, my students look younger and younger. I confess—every year I more and more feel this difference in our ages. So I don't date much anymore. I love teaching, except that I sometimes feel as though I have buried the best part of myself back in those wonderful years when we were a family—Otto, Mama, Papa, and me."

It was only a paragraph of words, but the texture of the conversation was so warm that their heads had drifted slowly together again. Mary wondered for a moment if it was really possible that she was in her own home having such a wonderful, profound conversation with another adult human being. It seemed as if the snow had returned her home to a past reality. But now another person was here saying how he felt and inducing such honesty from her that she felt it would not be possible ever to be dishonest again. Mary felt the air was charged this Christmas Eve. Even the light fixtures all had a special halo around them. Their faces were close. Their moods gigantic.

Alexis coughed once, then quieted.

Mary remonstrated with herself and straightened up against the back of her chair. So did Erick.

"Mary," Erick began again, after clearing his throat, "were it not for my teaching, I would be trapped forever in 1917, the year our family life died."

Mary thought for a moment before extending her hand to touch his own. "Erick, were it not for Alexis, I would be locked forever in 1926, the year of Tom's death, the year my family life died."

"Thanks be to the good Lord for my work at the university. Were it not for my students, I think I would not really want to get up most mornings."

"Which is precisely how I feel about Alexis."

Erick felt Christmas.

So did Mary.

Not venturing further faceward to risk either another kiss or rebuke, Erick nonetheless took her hand and raised it to his face. The moment the back of her fingers touched his jaw, Mary instinctively turned her hand upright and stroked his face. He, made bold by the subtle shadows and the lights, pressed his lips against her hand and held it as though he was lost in a kind of dream he had never known before. She did not immediately remove her hand, but when she did it was with a forcefulness that seemed to say that in spite of Christmas, things were moving far too fast for her. She would not recriminate him too much however, and taking the hand he had kissed, she reached to pat his leg. They smiled at each other. Then she stood, formally wishing him a merry Christmas.

"Merry Christmas to you, too, Mary Withers," Erick said, laughing.

Although Alexis had been quiet for the past half hour, she suddenly began coughing persistently in the adjoining room. Mary excused herself and quickly left to care for her. But in just a short while she returned, the medication having quieted Alexis's cough quite rapidly.

"Now, where were we?" asked Mary. "I believe I had just wished you a Merry Christmas."

"And I the same to you," said Erick.

During their warm volleys of confession and quiet evaluation, their coffee, through complete neglect, had gone completely cold. Mary picked up the cups and went into the kitchen, soon reemerging with two very steaming cups. "Forgive me, Erick, I'm all out of wassail this Christmas. In fact, I've been all out of wassail the past three Christmases. I'm out of butter cookies too. No matter! To be honest, I'm out of butter. I had to make a choice this week whether I would buy a coloring book for Alexis or bake her butter cookies. I chose the coloring book, since it's been so long since she's had one. I may not have chosen wisely."

Erick felt a kind of rebuke at her honesty. He knew she wasn't trying to appear poor to play on his sympathies. It was just the matter-of-fact way that Mary Withers explained things. Erick thought of his mother chopping walnuts and of that huge turkey hanging cold and ready on the Muellers' screened-in porch. Mary would have a very plain Christmas dinner, he was sure. It would be like most of her other dinners, warm with love and kept simple by thrift, yet he could picture it an elegant meal. But the Ephedrine, with its high cost, would take the place of the meal that Mary might have provided for herself and Alexis.

But there was little use noticing that Mary Withers was poorer than the Muellers. Mary hadn't noticed it. She was regal, somehow owning everything because she had a little girl and that little girl was still alive. Erick could tell this was Christmas enough for Mary Withers. And if the Ephedrine worked well, Erick might see in Mary's eyes the joy she would find in Alexis's eyes when she found the coloring book under that rail of a fir tree, which, having few branches, like Mary herself still seemed rich.

Erick remembered that his father had paid

two dollars for their tree. It seemed a scandal-
ous sum, but then the Muellers believed in
being reckless at Christmas. Yet for its pricey
presence in the Mueller house, the two-dollar
tree had a thin relative in the Witherses' house.
Both of them were equally proud trees, and
both of them had equally happy owners.

Erick was about to ask Mary if he could borrow her coal scoop to go out and try to liberate
his old truck so he could start home. But before
he could beg the shovel, Mary rose abruptly
and, setting her coffee cup down, turned in the
direction of Alexis's room. What Erick had not
even heard, Mary could not miss. The child in
the next room was once again laboring for
breath. Erick had been so entranced by Mary
Withers that he had pushed to the back of his
awareness the heavy breathing of a small child.
He was surprised, though, that he had not
heard it, for it was so painfully loud he didn't
see how the small child could live through such
convulsive gasping. Suddenly Erick could actually feel Alexis's sickness. Its desperation
chilled the air so lately warm with understanding. He had never realized till that moment that
sickness could be felt just as Christmas could be
felt. But sickness came as a thickening in the
air. Like the weight of things dreaded. Like the
bleak chill of a dying fire.

Ingrid Mueller, afraid of doing the wrong thing, fidgeted for two hours before doing anything. Then, even though it was late on Christmas Eve, she called the constable to report the mysterious, locally mailed letter. Next she called the postmaster. After making an apology for calling him at home so late, she asked if he had seen anyone resembling her description of Otto. She was disappointed in the information she received. No, there was no memory of a man in his midthirties coming into the post office to mail the Muellers' joyous and bewildering letter. Neither the constable nor the postmaster were of any help. Perhaps the greatest miracle of Christmas was that no one listened in on the phone lines during Ingrid's calls.

It was ten o'clock when Ingrid realized that Erick was still not back from the Witherses' house. While she always lit the tree candles at eight o'clock on Christmas Eve, it was ten-thirty before it even occurred to her that the wild events of the night had thrown tradition to the white winds. She wrung her hands in despair. She had the fidgets, as Hans would say, and began to pace the floor. When she finally stopped, she turned toward Hans and demanded, "Whatever is keeping Erick?"

Hans, having no idea, merely shrugged his shoulders. This shrug was so strong that it made the couch on which he was lying tremble. The shrug set Ingrid to pacing again.

After a moment or so of this, Hans said, "Oh, for goodness' sake, Ingrid, stop this pacing and go chop valnuts!"

"They are all chopped, Hans. Don't be so grumpy. It's Christmas."

"Ja, Ingrid, and it's der time of good cheer. Have a cup of vassail and go sit by the Tannenbaum and calm yourself."

"Hans, I can't just sit down. What if Erick has left the Witherses' and is now trapped somewhere freezing?"

"I'll tell you this, Ingrid, the lad is trapped at that vidow's house. He'll be home before long. Quit your valking about, vill you? Go get the turkey off the porch and start the giblets to boil. It'll give you something to do, and when you get the giblets to boil, the boy vill be home. Den you can light the candles."

But neither rolling out pie crusts nor starting the giblets to boil produced Erick.

Nothing ultimately helped Ingrid pull her frustrations together except pacing. So she started pacing once more.

"Ingrid, you're at it again, and this time you're wringing your hands too." Hans was beginning to feel a bit nervous himself. "Vhy don't you call over to that vidow's house and tell him it's time to come home?"

"Oh, Hans, do you think it would be all right?"

"No, Ingrid, I do not think it vould be all right, but I think it is all that vill settle you down."

"If it's not all right, I won't do it. I'd rather be nervous than improper."

It was a signal to Hans. He was not as stiff and had been feeling much recovered the last few days. He needed to move. Ingrid's homage to propriety must be paid, but Hans didn't mind at all being improper. He thought it was high time his Erick left the widow's house. It was all right to provide her the medicine that Dr. Drummond had ordered, but heaven only knew what else Erick might be snared into providing. And so, anxious to save his son from the "viles of the vild vidow," he crossed the floor Ingrid had all but worn out, picked up the receiver, and dialed the three-digit number of his eighth-of-a-ton coal customer. He turned the hand crank, ringing her bell. There was no immediate answer. The impatience that Ingrid exercised by walking the floor, Hans took out on the hand crank. Again he jerked the hand crank and then turned it once again for good measure.

He heard two receivers click up in turn while he waited for the "Vithers vidow." He knew that his Christmas Eve call would be a kind of present to both Janet Breckenridge and Mabel Cartwright. He turned the hand crank, and the Witherses' phone rang yet again. At last he got a response.

"Hello. Withers residence, Erick Mueller speaking!"

"Erick, this is your fader. Are you going to spend the night at the Vitherses' house?"

"Papa, please. You know Janet and Mabel are listening. Please, Janet and Mabel, I want you to do two things. First of all, you mustn't tell everyone in the parish that I'm spending the night with Mary Withers. I'm not. You can tell them that my truck became bogged down in a drift while I was making a delivery for Dr. Drummond. Now, it's Christmas Eve. Will you get off the line and let me talk to my father?"

It was a miracle. Both Erick and his father heard two distinct clicks, and they both were made warm by the feeling that they were alone on the line.

"Erick, did you get the truck stuck?"

"Yes, Papa, I did! I was going to borrow Mary's shovel and dig it out and try to get home, but now Mary's little Alexis is very sick, and I don't know if I should abandon her right now."

"Abandon her?" Suddenly Hans was all but shouting into the receiver. "Vhat about your poor mother and me? You don't seem to mind abandoning us. You know your mother vill vait till you are here to pour the vassail and light the candles. So vhen are you coming home, boy?"

"Papa, the little girl is very sick. I can't come home right now."

"Erick, you are not a doctor. I say you come home now!"

"Papa, ask Mama if maybe we could light the candles tomorrow night after our big Christmas dinner."

Erick heard the receiver slam down. He could tell his father was out of control. How well he knew the strength of Hans' tantrums. He was glad that he was far beyond his father's reach. When Hans became livid, Erick simply left the room, or the house, if necessary. He never forgot that horrible scene with Otto so many years ago. He wanted no such incident ever to occur again.

Hans stood by the phone shaking with anger. Then suddenly he felt ashamed, and the blood from his face drained. His self-reflection caused him to see himself as he was, and remembering that it was Christmas, he turned to his wife and said meekly, "Ingrid, you call the boy. Tell him I'm sorry. I don't vant him to try to come home in this storm. He might never make it."

Dutifully, Ingrid walked to the phone. With a kind of grace, she rang the number and found herself working to repair Hans' damage. Before she was ready, she heard her son speaking so quietly he was most unlike his father.

"Withers residence, Erick Mueller speaking."

Ingrid paused for a moment and bit her lower lip, not knowing exactly how to repair the former conversation.

"Erick, your father is sorry for his outburst."

"*Nein, nein!* It is not for you to say, Ingrid," protested Hans, still standing near the phone. He grabbed the receiver out of her hand. "I am der *alte* fool. I vill answer like I should have in der first place. Boy, forgive me, if you can."

Ingrid stood bewildered. So did Erick, far away in the Witherses' house. He heard his parents, and above all his father, doing something he could never have imagined him doing. Erick's dumbfounded state left him silent for so long that Hans thought for a moment that he might have lost the connection.

"Son, are you still there?"

"Yes, Papa, I'm still here."

"Then, son, dis I beg you. Forgive me. I am an *alte* fool. I am sorry. Say you pardon me, all right?"

"Of course, Papa. There is nothing to pardon."

Hans and Erick were both quiet for a moment. Hans, glorying in the warmth that his own repentance had engendered. Eric, loving the open way his father had just begged his forgiveness. It was Hans who first broke the awkward telephone silence.

"Vill you be able to get the truck unstuck?"

"I don't know, Papa. I'll try, but Alexis Withers is so sick, and Dr. Drummond is stuck at Caslin's Dairy."

"Vell, boy, do vhat you vill. Ve can light your mudder's candles tomorrow evening after dinner and before dose mince meat pies."

"Yes, Papa!"

"The snow vill be easier to deal mitt in der daylight, am I right?'

"Of course, Papa."

"Son, there is one thing I must tell you. Your mother vanted to vait till you were home . . . but I cannot. I could vish you vere here, so I could tell you face to face. But, son, ve believe Otto is not only alive but somevhere here in King of Prussia."

"Papa, whatever makes you say such a thing?"

"Vell, boy, ve got a letter from him today! It's *wunderbar*! The letter was postmarked here in town. I vould give anything to find him before Christmas."

The news was so stunning that Erick was speechless.

So were Janet Breckenridge and Mabel Cartwright.

"Erick, are you still there?"

"Papa! Papa! This is marvelous. Tomorrow we must set another place at the table. This town is not so big that we cannot find him if he is to be found. Papa, I'll come home as soon as Alexis is better. As soon as I get the truck unstuck."

"The point is, boy, that you must not risk yourself in the dark and cold. Be careful. You know how people can become disoriented in these storms."

"I will, Papa. God bless you! Merry Christmas!"

"Merry Christmas, boy!"

Hans hung up the receiver. He was smiling.

He wasn't altogether sure just why he was smiling, but somehow he knew that something was about to happen. But what was it? What was this glorious impending? And why was it that when something wonderful was about to happen, the mood of the mystery arrives so far ahead of the mystery itself? What was it that hid in the snows of King of Prussia, Pennsylvania?

Hans wasn't sure. He wasn't sure of anything.

Ingrid slipped up behind him while he stood at the phone. She fanned the fingers of both hands in a kind of coronation ritual. It was Christmas and time to bestow the best gift she had given Hans in many a year. From Ingrid's long, graceful fingers a thin silver chain fell over Hans' heavy head and came to rest around his thick neck. Hans understood. It was Otto's chain. Just wearing it gave him a huge rush of emotion. He used his thumbs to wipe the tears from his ruddy cheeks.

Ingrid smiled.

She kissed the cross at the end of the chain.

Then she kissed her husband.

She ran her fingers between the thin chain and the graying hairs sticking out from Hans' shirt. This chain was nothing less than the gift of the Magi: a present so weighted with hope and promise it could only be given at Christmas.

Mary stayed so long in Alexis's bedroom that Erick began to feel odd in the crushing emptiness of the front room. He took it upon himself to feed the potbellied stove. The fire in the iron pit had waned to the point that the poker seemed unable to stir it back to life. Erick mixed the black lumps of all he was adding with the glowing embers of the coal Mary had put in an hour earlier. He felt a strange distraction in the practical thing he was trying to do. He wanted to do something to help Mary in the agony he knew she was enduring while he put coal in the stove. Mary really needed him, yet he felt so stupid and useless.

He could hear Alexis gasping for breath. It was frightening to hear the child in such distress. He tried not to listen. He had tried every minute to believe it would soon be over and Mary would come back into the living room

107

smiling and announcing that Alexis was doing better. But no such announcement came. Nor did Mary come back.

He took his place beyond the stove and waited. He rose every so often, walking to the door of Alexis's room. He wanted to break in and interrupt the private world of mother and child. But instead he sat down again. Then he got up and repeated the whole process.

The single focus of this early Christmas Eve was now muddled by his father's revelation. He thought of Otto, mostly of Otto, then only of Mary. The two faces—one of his estranged brother and the other of Mary Withers—occupied the alternating focus of his mind. *Otto!* he thought, *where are you? Can you really be so near? Can you, after having been so far away, so long? Mary, dear Mary! Will the ordeal of your child destroy the whole serenity of all we have shared? Would the death of your child destroy your peace of mind forever? Why am I out here, stuck in the snow, unable to help find Otto and also unable to help poor Mary keep Alexis alive? Yet why should I think of her as poor?*

He felt for the first time in the evening that he really ought to leave, that he wanted to leave. Yet somehow he hated to bother Mary, even to ask her where she kept the coal shovel he needed to free the truck from its white prison. He didn't know exactly what she was dealing with inside the bedroom, but he just didn't feel right crashing in there.

He stood up and walked toward the Shaker coatrack inside the main door. Reaching out for his coat, he took it from the oak peg. He was about to put it on and see if he could locate the coal scoop without asking Mary's permission. He was determined to see if he could get the truck out of the snow so that when the child was better—if the child got better—and Mary gave him permission, he could head for home. In his mind even that seemed wrong, for the intensity of the storm left him no guarantees that the old truck could burst through the drifts that barred every road between the Witherses' place and the edge of town. Just as he swung the coat around his lower back and started inserting an arm into the thick, heavy sleeve, Mary called to him from Alexis's doorway.

"Erick, I feel I must move Alexis closer to the fire. Could you help me?"

Without reply, Erick quickly replaced the coat on the peg and hurried into the bedroom from which Mary's voice had come. The room was lit by a weak bulb which seemed an apology for real light. But even the scant illumination brought Erick face-to-face with a kind of specter he was unprepared to meet. Little Alexis, who earlier that day had appeared so perky and alive, looked like a gargoyle in pain.

It did not last long, but Erick immediately felt a sense of the deep mystery. Perhaps it was the darkness of the room. Perhaps it was the oddly skeletal look of the child as she struggled to take each breath. Then, too, there was Caspian, whose yellow eyes seemed to capture all the stingy light that was available.

But this eerie first impression rapidly gave way to a noble study of the truth.

Alexis's thin chest heaved upward in a ghastly attempt to get her lungs to take in enough air to keep them going. The child's tiny mouth was open wide in an attempt to breathe. The nightstand held the medicine that Erick had brought, the medicine that had been his right of passage, his real reason for even being there. The small nightstand seemed a kind of high altar, which held the stuff of life. Mary looked like an abbess, faithful in her adoration of that single ritual that furnished life to the only thing that really mattered to her.

Mary had mixed the Ephedrine in what had earlier been a glass of clear water, leaving it a milky solution. It was most apparent to Erick that when Alexis had quit strangling enough to take it, Mary—as she so often had seen Dr. Drummond do—ladled the liquid down a very small throat caught in spasms. Erick could never fathom the marvelous meaning of motherhood, but he understood how this beautiful child could only have life so long as Mary made it possible. Here in the dimly lit inner sanctum was occurring a homespun miracle. He feared the room, for what was happening here was a simplicity majestic. Erick saw the room as a place where the angels might build a little monument to all that is most noble in the human spirit. Yet he knew that those who acted out the small drama would be too involved in keeping their ritual to measure the grandeur of it all.

Surely, thought Erick, *this child will live. This child must live. To reward this mother, the keeper of life, with death would be enough to abolish Christmas forever and make God's fairness seem questionable throughout the world.*

"Erick, please, can you lift her up and carry her to the couch out by the stove?"

Could he? Of course he could. But should he do it? He distrusted his demeanor. Would he be gentle enough? Could he handle Mary's greatest treasure with her same tenderness? No, none could do that but Mary. What right did he have? He had too little long-term investment in the child's struggle to have earned the right to serve. Still, he could do it. He must. He did. Now he cared. Now he helped. Now he determined to be careful not to trip.

He knew he was making too much of Mary's request. Erick renounced his bogus feelings of melodrama. The little room that earlier seemed a pageant of life dwindled to what it really was—a ward of desperation. It was even, as he knew Mary saw it, a place to do good and not evil. It was a sickroom. Nothing more! Erick bent over the tiny bed and scolded the white pet. "Out of the way, Caspian!"

The cat obeyed, and the coal man, more than the university professor, scooped the child into his arms. He was amazed at how light she was. Could such a great struggle really be occurring in this little form? Could these forty pounds or so of life be the focus of the doting love of a simple woman who lived and served God alone on the outskirts of King of Prussia, Pennsylvania?

Mary examined Erick's deliberate movement. He seemed a reply to the fear that managed her hope. Christmas could not erase the pain of her motherhood, but the God who created Christmas with a baby was using her own child to help her remember she was not alone. Erick was there. With swift steps he carried Alexis to the couch. Caspian—in a kind of congenial defiance of the desperation—followed along at Erick's heels. Ever so gently Erick laid Alexis on the couch, and Mary quickly covered her with the quilt.

"Mama," said Alexis, "Mr.—" she could not go on. She had to stop and wait while her sickness crushed her ribs into a cruel spasm. A tremendous rattling cough exploded from her chest, silencing the room with its fury. When her gasping subsided a few moments later, she finished her words, taking up exactly where she had left off. ". . . Mueller is a strong man. Will he—" Another spasm shook her. This time the assault was so strong it looked as though she would never get the air to catch again in her breast. But at last it did, and she shuddered and continued. ". . . stay till Christmas?"

"If he needs to, darling," Mary said, answering Alexis far more quickly than she could ask. "You mustn't try to talk. Just rest."

Alexis closed her eyes, but not before reaching out toward Caspian. As her fingers closed in the soft white fur, another spasm overcame her, and when the coughing ceased, she released the cat and closed her eyes.

"Erick, would you bring the medicine on the nightstand?"

In an instant Erick obeyed.

"I need to stay here by Alexis in case I get the chance to give her a little more of the Ephedrine. I'm afraid if I leave her, I may miss the opportunity. I need you to do one other thing for me, if you will. I hate to press this upon you, but would you go the kitchen and get the copper teakettle, fill it with water at the sink, and set it on the stove? Be sure it's the copper teakettle. That's the only one I use eucalyptus oil in. The white one I keep for cooking and scalding the dishes."

Again Erick complied.

"There's a small brown bottle of eucalyptus oil on the kitchen windowsill. Would you bring it in and put a few drops of the oil in the kettle? When it starts steaming, it will help Alexis breathe."

Erick was off yet a third time and came back with the small bottle as requested. Removing the cap from the bottle, he gently tapped a few drops out of the bottle, letting them fall into the kettle. Then he set the bottle aside and waited. They both waited. Mary waited for the next small window of opportunity to give Alexis more medicine. Every quarter of an hour, the child's struggle seemed almost to end. At such times Mary quickly propped her little head up and gave her some more of the medicine. Erick almost believed the child was about to be through the nightmarish cycle of rising and gasping and then sinking down again. Erick waited for Mary's next request, only no request came.

But leaving was out of the question. He would feel horrible abandoning Mary in such an hour. Many things went through Erick's mind. He had earlier thought of marriage but rebuked himself for such a hurried, capricious thought. *But that's how love is*, he assured himself. *When you first taste the delight, you cannot help but wonder if it is only the first step toward something more enduring.*

Now, however, he had been to the inner sanctum of all mercy. He had seen a mother and child locked in mutual dependency. He had seen love struggle with pain and watched love win. He had seen a need so demanding that he no longer believed he was equal enough to Mary Withers to even consider the proposition. She was able to face the beast, and if it could be stared down, she would manage it. But he could not. He taught mathematics. He was unskilled in caring when the stakes were so high. Mary had grown in his estimation while he but shrunk in his own esteem. Still, he resolved to offer her his full commitment in the struggle she could not abandon.

Erick often forgot during the next two hours the severity of Alexis's ordeal. But Mary never presumed. Her daughter's real condition could never be taken for granted. Erick knew that the moment Mary relaxed, Alexis would be in real danger. But Erick was too new to it all, and the longer Alexis fought and won, the more he believed she would go on winning, however torturous her gasping. After Erick had seen Alexis struggle he found his mind wandering, thinking about a million things. Was it really Christmas? The odd gaiety of Christmas had been swallowed up in wearisome desperation. He wondered for a moment if any of this was real, and if it were, what in the world was he doing in the midst of it?

The teakettle was boiling. Tiny drops of eucalyptus had buried the woodsy odor of the thin Christmas tree in what smelled more like a hospital corridor. Still the steam, laced with the menthol aroma, was somehow friendly to the little girl. And the boiling kettle vibrating on the stovetop reminded Erick to get up and stoke the fire again. It was while looking up from the coal scuttle that he heard something fall—something tin, like a second coal scuttle—somewhere else in the house. But where in the house? Beyond the door with the heavy buffet wedged across the front of it? Heavy buffet across a door—why?

In spite of Alexis's needs, Erick knew that Mary heard it too.

"What was that?" he asked.

"What?" asked Mary.

"That noise!"

Mary knew that it was time to stop her pretending. "I don't know," she replied, "but I heard it earlier in the day."

"Mary, how big is this house?"

"There are four more rooms beyond that door," she said, nodding toward the door behind the buffet. Suddenly Mary felt she owed

Erick an explanation. "I can't afford to heat the whole house, so I have sealed off the back rooms for the last three winters. It really does save on the coal bill."

"I understand," he said, "but is it possible someone could be back there? Maybe there's a raccoon holing up there. It could be anything . . . or anyone. Shhh . . ." Erick said suddenly, as though he suddenly heard some noise coming from the sealed area.

They both grew quiet, listening intently. All was silent.

"I thought I heard something back there just before you arrived, but I wasn't sure."

"Didn't you check it out?" asked Erick, bewildered.

"No, I went to the basement, which runs under both halves of this old place, but . . . no, I didn't check it out. Alexis was just beginning to get sick, so I shoved this buffet across the upstairs door and bolted the basement door."

"But why didn't you call the constable?" Erick probed.

"Erick, I don't know . . . I guess I just made a deal with my fears. It's awful having to fear what may be in the back of your own house. I really wasn't all that certain I had heard anything, so I tried to forget it, maybe to talk myself out of it. But not really having convinced myself, I shoved this buffet across the door."

"The thing must weigh three hundred pounds. However did you manage to move it?"

"I ... I don't know. It seemed important somehow. It never occurred to me to wonder if I could do it. I just did it." It was only in the wake of Erick's wonder at her superhuman feat that it occurred to Mary that she herself should have been amazed.

All of a sudden Alexis heaved upward in a horrendous spasm. Mary deftly changed foes, coming again to focus on Alexis's needs and not the other possible enemy that might be in some other part of her small and insecure empire.

"Stay with Alexis. I must go and check this out."

"Be careful, Erick," said Mary as she swabbed the girl's brow with a wet washrag. "Mabel Cartwright told me she had seen the back chimney smoking the last couple of nights. She assumed I had been using the stove in the back part of the house, but I have not used it since November. It was Mabel's odd comment, I think, that caused me to overreact."

"Well, I'm going to go check it out."

Mary said nothing but shuddered and leaned against the wall. She closed her eyes, but the closure could not prevent a tear from slipping out. She shuddered again.

Erick could see she was afraid.

"Erick, I'm so frightened," she said, opening

her eyes and trying to appear confident. "I have nothing to offer you to help you defend yourself."

"This will work very fine," he said, picking up the poker.

It was exactly the weapon that she had chosen earlier in the evening when she had descended the stairs.

"I think I'll just move this buffet away from the door and go check out those empty rooms." Erick began to heave with his shoulder against one end of the heavy piece of furniture.

"No! Please! Erick, please don't move the buffet. I'll feel much safer if you leave it where it is. Take the stairs and enter the other part of the house through the basement. The electricity is off in the back part of the house as well, but there's a lantern in the basement."

Then he kissed her on top of the head. He really had no right to do so. He did it partly because he didn't know what else to do and partly because it seemed all right to do it. "I'll be back shortly," he said.

But somehow he wasn't all that sure he would.

Erick, holding the poker in one hand, lit a candle and started down the basement stairs. In contrast to the electric lights upstairs, the candle seemed dim illumination. He stopped on the second tread to allow his eyes time to adjust to the meager light cast by the candle flame. Then he went on down the stairs and came at last to the basement. He found the lantern and was pleased to feel the weight of it as he took it from a wooden peg jutting out from the side of the coal bin. It told him at once that the lantern was full of kerosene. He tripped the spring mechanism, raised the globe, and touched the candle to the wick. The wick jumped instantly to flame, and he lowered the globe and adjusted the thumbscrew until the glare dimmed to a steady bright flame. Then he blew out the candle and, holding the lantern ahead of him, advanced to the wall that separated the two parts of the basement. He paused at the connecting doorway, then, reaching out to the hasp that kept the door secure, he removed the bolt that Mary had placed there only hours before. He opened the door and peered into the dark. Once more he paused. The light of the lantern was steady, but the shadows that fell behind him were as eerie as the boxes and storage cases that lined the shelves.

Advancing across the floor, he climbed the stairs. They creaked under his weight, and he paused when he reached the door at the top. He placed his hand on the doorknob that would allow him to pass into the rear of Mary Withers' house. Now he was really frightened. He gripped the iron handle of the poker with part of his free hand and still found grip enough to turn the doorknob. Stepping into the room, he closed the basement door behind him.

One thing immediately impressed him. The room was dark but warm. He tried the light switch, but no light came on. Mary, true to her word, had taken the fuses from the fuse box that controlled this part of the house. He advanced through the kitchen, stealthily measuring his steps, but the floor, like the staircase, creaked noisily. If anybody was here, they would surely know he was present.

Then he set the lantern on the small round table in one corner of the unused kitchen and waited for his eyes to adjust. The stove in the kitchen, which was keeping all three rooms warm, was ablaze. The coal scuttle was full of coal. He opened the door to the stove, and the fire in the belly of the cheerful heater cast a host of shadows all through the hall and fell fully on a door that he presumed led to the spare bedroom.

Holding the lantern in front of him, he went directly to the room, cautiously opening the door. No one was there. The bed was made, and yet it somehow had the distinct look of having been slept in. Erick went back to the small table and picked up the lantern. Then he went back into the hallway and closed the door on the stove, shutting down the dancing, amber shadows. The lantern light was steadier but lacked the glow of the open stove.

Unable to make anything of the empty but warm house, Erick was baffled. He walked to the kitchen door that led outside. When he opened the door, the relentless snow swirled in. The cold sting of the flakes burned his warm face, but gently. The snow obliterated everything. There was only a swirl about his lantern and not much light. Holding his arm over his brow to shelter his eyes, he tried to see out into the night. It was useless. At least a foot of snow had accumulated, and the thickness of the falling gloom produced only an amber wall of orange snow.

He turned to go back into the house ... but wait ... what was that? There in the snow were footprints that began just outside the door and hurried away into the night. He suddenly realized that his advance up the steps must have frightened whoever had been making the back part of Mary's house his own. He pulled the outside door shut and bolted it.

In but a moment or so he was back in Mary Withers' room.

"What in the world was all that noise I heard?" Mary was desperate.

"Mary, I don't know how to tell you this, but Mabel Cartwright was right. Someone has been squatting in the back of your house. The fire is going even now, and the rooms are warm as toast. I scared off someone who fled into the night when he heard me coming up the stairs."

"Erick, this is eerie. I can't believe it could have happened without my being aware of it."

"Mary, how's Alexis doing?" asked Erick, aware that the ordeal of a sinister guest—awful as it was—was only one of Mary's concerns.

"She's resting much quieter in the last few minutes," said Mary as she continued to hover over the couch that had become Alexis's bed.

"Mary, I wonder if you would be opposed to putting the fuses back in the panel and lighting

123

up that part of the house. A little illumination can scare away a lot of evil."

"The fuses are all in a little box sitting on top of the panel."

Erick needed only her nod to go into the rear section of the house and set it alive with light. When illumination had returned, Erick decided to investigate everything that the scant light of his first trip had prevented him from seeing. Nothing in the closet could have belonged to Mary and Alexis. After a thorough search, he came up empty. Then he bent over and, looking under the bed, found a five-cent cigar box labeled "El Producto" cigars. *Cheap Havana tobacco*, he thought to himself. Drawing the cigar box out from under the bed, he removed the rubber band that held the lid down and opened the box. He was surprised that Mary kept such impressive relics in such a cheap box. Among the other artifacts were a solid gold pocket watch and a receipt for a stock transaction, dated that very day. The receipt was made in the amount of sixty-three dollars! He thought it must be Mary's survival money—the kitty out of which she paid for her eighth ton of coal every two weeks. But where would Mary get any stocks to sell?

On down in the box was a Swiss army knife and three new monogrammed handkerchiefs. The monogram, *O.M.*, was very nice, the kind of initialing that is usually done in the swank men's shops of Manhattan. It must have been a box of Tom's old things that Mary kept for sentimental reasons. No, that was crazy! Mary's husband's things should have been monogrammed with *T.W.* for Tom Withers. Light flooded his mind at once. *O.M.* were his brother's initials. The insight came even as he reached the bottom of the box. Pressed into one corner lay a photo taken some fifteen years earlier. Four people smiled genuinely for the camera. The young boy on the left was Erick himself.

"Mary, Mary!" Erick said, running against the door sealed by the buffet. Mary was so preoccupied with Alexis she didn't hear him call her name. Realizing the door would not give way, he retraced his way across the sealed rooms and flew down the back stairs into the basement. Running through the hallway and up the stairs, he exploded into Mary's presence. "Look at this," Erick insisted, thrusting the rubber-banded cigar box at her.

Mary, somewhat taken aback by his explosive entry into the room and his nearly mandatory order, tentatively reached out. "What is it, Erick?"

"Open it!"

Again his eagerness somewhat unnerved her, but she obeyed. When her fingers had wound the rubber band around themselves, she lifted the lid. "I don't understand. What is all this stuff? Where did you get it?"

"Mary, look at the photograph! There ... on the bottom of the box."

She rifled through the heavier paraphernalia on the top and, coming to the bottom of the box, slid the picture, on command, out from under the weightier trifles on top. She moved the picture closer to her face and studied it.

"I don't know these people. Should I? Who are they?"

"That's me on the end ... fifteen years ago. Mary, I believe your mysterious, unseen, unwelcome boarder may be my brother, the second from the left. Mary, I must leave you for a while. The storm is severe, and whoever has been living in the back part of your house—whoever left that box—I frightened away when I entered the kitchen a moment ago. I know he left the house. He left his footprints on the stoop as he fled into the night.

"I'll try not to be gone for too long. But if it is Otto, he is out there in the most desperate of storms. I must find him before the storm obliterates his tracks."

Mary nodded. Alexis was not doing well, and she knew it. But there was something so desperate about Erick's demeanor that she could not say no to him. She added a weak smile of permission to her nod.

Once again Erick kissed her on top of the

head, even though he had earlier said he would never do it without her permission. It was a kiss of immense promise, yet utterly chaste, nearly sacred in its intent. He added to the kiss the brief touching of her hair. His touch, like his kiss, was a kind of commitment. Whether he touched, kissed, or delivered coal, he did it all with a sense of commitment—a sense that his every deed was offered, not as a stranger or a client, but as a man in love. It was not just love he gave to Mary, it was romance with the art of being alive.

Erick followed his touch with an abrupt turn. In but a minute he was clad in his mackinaw, the chin-strapped hat, and his triple-latched rubber galoshes. As he passed the front closet, he grabbed an armful of clothes hangers and thrust the thick sleeve of his mackinaw through the lot of them. Then, with the hangers up and down his arm, he retraced his basement route, picking up the lantern on the way through and hurrying on up the stairs and into the kitchen. He took a match from Mary's matchbox and struck its sulfur head on the sandpaper strip. The match broke into a small fire, which ignited the lantern wick into a greater fire. Then Erick, without even pausing, turned to the door, opened it, and stepped out into the night.

It was past midnight on Christmas Eve. And

if weather alone could create Christmas, it was indeed the season. The snow fell as eagerly as it had earlier in the day. There was no up, no down, no north, no south. There was only a blaze of cold confetti, vaulting, descending, swirling. Into this bewildering, befuddling assault on his senses, Erick crunched forward, an orange-lantern seeker studying the rapidly disappearing footprints. Erick knew they would soon be gone, and worse than that, within half an hour his own footprints would also be filled in, and he would be unable to use his own new trail to find his way back to the house. He remembered Jake Williams, who had frozen to death in the blizzard of '20. They had found him only a few blocks from his home. He had apparently wandered about in a field, killed by just such a whiteout made by the Atlantic air in Pennsylvania.

He must hurry in order to complete the round trip in less than half an hour. Walking as briskly as possible, he frequently looked back, trying to mark the moment he could no longer see the orange light of Mary Withers' house. When he had gone that far, though he had no idea how far it was, he turned and thrust the first hanger endwise into the snow. It was a crude but life-saving marker sticking there, with its crooked head facing in the direction where the amber windows were still fairly visible. Every fifty paces or so he repeated this odd ritual of snow-hangering his way into the relentless wilderness. He soon realized he had used up most of the hangers, and still there was no sign of the man he pursued. Even the footprints were becoming harder to follow as the wind had nearly obliterated them.

Mercifully he arrived at the fencerow. Here the drifting was less formidable and the walking much easier. The footprints of the man he sought were more distinct here than in the open field behind the house. Within fifteen or twenty feet he stumbled over an eroding hay bale the neighboring farmhands had left too close to the fence. It was so covered with white snow it hardly resembled a hay bale.

Erick stepped over it and turned to jab an upright hanger into it, but it wouldn't go in. *The hay must be frozen*, he thought to himself. Then he noticed that there was a piece of tartan wool sticking out of the clump. Even in the stingy light of the lantern, it betrayed its red scotched-plaid fabric with a bit of a tassel. A hay bale in tartan?

Confused by this incongruity, he sought to inspect it even closer. It made no sense at all, so he tested it, nudging it with his shoe. Nothing would come of this cold conundrum.

Finally, Erick kicked at the odd clump of snow.

It moaned, like some kind of animal freezing unwillingly in the night storm. But this was no animal—what of this scarf? Erick kneeled and brushed away the snow. "You're alive!" he cried in the swirling confusion. "You're a man!" He set the lantern in the cold snow that wept in thaw at the heat of the lantern. Then he brushed away all the snow. The white-clotted stocking cap was dry, and the slicker beneath the scarf had kept the snow from freezing the man's face. Still, the man wore far too little to be plodding in this blizzard. He had not enough clothing to keep him alive in the confusing fields where all direction and distance were engulfed in meaningless wandering.

Erick lifted up the man's shoulders, propping him against the fence post near the place where he had fallen. "What are you doing out on a night like this?" At once Erick saw the truth. The tracks he had been pursuing ended at this clump. There were no tracks beyond the fallen man. This hapless freezing soul was the object of his pursuit. This was Mary's uninvited boarder. This was . . . no, it could not be . . . not Otto! Not here in the middle of a blizzard! No!

Erick allowed the lantern light to pass near the face. Who lay here? What familiarity would not declare itself? What had the years stolen from a longing brother and hidden in a snowy field? What prodigal ever went to war and came home in a snow globe, desperate and dead? The man made feeble by his near escape and the encroaching cold had escaped with too little clothing. The night was so thick and white and frigid he could not long survive. Erick knew he must test all his suspicions. He spoke but one word, confidently, loudly, and directly. "OTTO!"

The man opened his eyes. He moaned a kind of agreement.

The lantern light brought together two odd faces, nourished by a kind of familiarity that nothing could erase. The near-frozen face peered through the lantern light. The half-frozen man raised his arm slowly and touched his cheek. "Erick?"

"Brother!" repeated Erick. What eleven years of searching could not effect, the snow had revealed—hope!

The glazed eyes of the vagabond shut. Otto slumped backwards against the fence post. Erick could not bear to face what his mind said was too late to reverse. Otto was dying! Or was he? He was so malnourished he appeared gaunt. He was not all that far from the house, so it must be that his physical hunger had joined with the cold to bring him down. Erick was in no sense robust, yet he picked Otto up fairly easily. Was Otto light merely because of Erick's joy? No, he was light because he must have been starving for a while. Erick draped Otto's thin body over the broad shoulder pads of his mackinaw, then picked up the lantern and began to retrace his own footprints. Passing hanger after hanger, he realized those thin wire sentinels were performing just as he hoped they would. Once his fading footprints turned from the fencerow to cross the fields, it was only the hangers, with their crooked necks always pointing toward the unseen house, that kept him going in the right direction. The snow was deep, and Otto, who had earlier felt too emaciated to be heavy, now seemed to weigh a ton. Erick stumbled forward, lifting his feet as high as he could to step over the deep snow. Yet his feet kept scrubbing that snow because of the extra weight he was carrying.

The effort of his rescue caused him to gulp in broad drafts of knifing air. His lungs burned from the frigid air.

There were several times he thought of laying Otto down and resting before taking him up again, yet he did not. He was transfixed by the fear that Otto's life was so much in the balance that he dare not rest. Time must be saved if Otto was to be saved. Pausing to catch his breath was not an option.

Wind tore at his face. Biting shards of ice blew into his eyes as he squinted into the darkness.

Crunch! Lunge! Stumble!

The walk cannot have consumed more than a quarter of an hour, yet his struggle threatened to burst his lungs with each intake of the frigid air. His chest heaved, demanding he breathe in large gulps. His legs rose, fell, locked, flexed, pumped, ground their way toward that place where the fire burned and warmth beckoned.

How grateful he was that when the hangers stopped he could see the windows of Mary's home shining like those of a lighthouse. The swirling snow could not conceal that light. He thanked God even as he prayed for God to help him make it. The house could not be more than a hundred yards ahead, yet the snow was deep, the task grueling. He could, he must. Stepping, stumbling, still scrubbing the high drifts, he moved on carrying his precious cargo, often falling but always falling forward. He remembered from his college literature class the tale of Jean Valjean in *Les Miserables* carrying the wounded Mario through the sewers of Paris. Only that was just a story, and this was real life. Why he thought of it he didn't know. Now the house was close. Otto would live. They would make it.

Then, struggling for stamina, he dropped the lantern! He did not even try to retrieve it. Its flame sizzled and died behind him, smothered in white. He did not look back. It would be there in the spring. He hurried on toward the back of the house, for in his state of sheer exhaustion, he didn't think he could reach the front.

The house was but fifty yards away. Then thirty. Now, at last, he knew he would make it. Stumbling onto the stoop, he swung the door open, and the outside elements met the insistent warmth of a coal fire. The rush of warm air caught the fragile snowflakes and drove them by their swirling millions back outside. Erick closed the door behind him.

"Mary, Mary," he gasped weakly.

He paused, gathered his breath, and bellowed, "Mary!"

"Erick! Are you all right?" came her beautiful voice, made distant by a wall and a heavy antique buffet.

"I'm all right, Mary. I found him. I found Otto!"

"What?" Mary called. "What?" she insisted a second time, even louder.

"Otto! I found him!"

Mary heard him. Not just what he said, but the confidence and joy with which he said it.

Then Erick heard a dull scraping sound and felt the oak flooring tremble. Mary was moving the buffet, sliding it away from the door. He could hear her fumbling with the key ring. Then the door directly ahead of him opened, and the two halves of the house came together. The rooms which Mary and Alexis knew became one with the rooms that had held terror and fear.

Erick stood before Mary holding a large bundle draped across his shoulder. Erick, a thin monarch. A man who faced fear and made it retreat. A man who could exorcise the demons from a house, and yet who would deny his courage both by his demeanor and his casual way of solving large problems. If Mary Withers had any doubt about being in love with Erick, they were swallowed up in the vision of a man void of fear holding a snowy, dripping bundle of responsibility.

"Mary, may I put him on the bed in this back bedroom? He's dripping and will likely make a mess of things."

"Erick, please! Don't even ask." Mary grabbed a little whisk broom and brushed most of the water and snow from the comatose bundle. Erick removed Otto from his shoulder and steadied his limp form upon an oak chair. In this temporary position he removed the slicker and tartan scarf. Otto looked dead.

"Can you imagine being out in a storm like this with so little on?" Erick asked Mary the question, yet his question was only desperation talking to itself. "Mary, would you peel back the covers on the bed?"

It was an order of sorts, yet Mary quickly responded. Erick pulled off Otto's pants and

shirt, both of them cold and fringed with dampness where the warmth of Otto's body had first
met the snow that had all but claimed his life.
Otto lay there, a near naked man, while Mary
quickly pulled the covers back over him. Then
she ran to the nearby hall closet and pulled out
two old blankets.

"Oh, Erick, I'm so ashamed for you to see
these ragged old bedclothes. I always meant to
replace them..."

"Mary, never you mind. They're fine. Just
fine!" Erick said, opening the folded blankets
and throwing them across his brother.

It was only then, when the first step of rescue
was over, that the two of them stopped to study
the great gift that had fallen on King of Prussia,
Pennsylvania. The restoration of brothers—the
homecoming of hope! It had fallen like the
snow, born in snow, preserved in snow. It had
come like those rich gifts once laid by the Magi
before a wondering new mother in a long-ago
Mediterranean stable.

Then Erick bent over the silent form and
kissed the cold forehead.

Mary could not hold back the tears, and
turning from Erick, she wept at the beautiful
sight of brother meeting brother. There was
utter glory in such a kiss.

Suddenly Mary got hold of her sentiments.
"Is he alive?"

Erick acted as though he would feel his wrist to see if there was a pulse. But no. He did not need to. He knew.

"Mary, he's alive, alive, alive and home, home, home!"

"Mommy! Mommy!" A thin but positive voice came from the next room. "Has Santa come yet?" It was Alexis. It was the first real words she had spoken in five hours that were not interrupted by the tenuous gasping of her illness. Mary could tell that Alexis was doing much better now and was no longer fighting a moment by moment struggle for life.

Even so, Mary knew she must not neglect her responsibilities. "Excuse me, Erick, I must get back to Alexis." He nodded in approval, and Mary left the room. Now each of them had a commitment to make the night a season of miracles in the midst of the raging elements. *Erick and Mary, who are we? What has God given us to share?* Mary was thoughtful. *We are mentors to each other on how to deal with things mysterious and hard. Yet each of us has borrowed hope from the other's mission.* Mary dutifully swirled the Ephedrine in a small glass and waited for her opportunity to make Christmas yield the kind of hope and good cheer it was famous for.

Erick would not take Otto's near brush with death as anything less than a visitation of joy. While Mary warmed the solution for her daughter, Erick warmed coffee for his brother.

"Shall we call your parents and tell them Otto is alive and home?" Mary asked Erick in the kitchen.

"Yes, yes," Erick said eagerly, almost racing for the phone. He picked up the earpiece and took the crank in his hand, fully intending to wake up old Mrs. Samuels. Then he stopped, looked fixedly at the frost-blasted windows, and hung the earpiece back on the hook.

"No, no! I've a better idea. Otto will rest a bit and regain his strength, and then I'm going to give Hans and Ingrid Mueller the best Christmas gift they have ever had, delivered to their door in the cab of their own coal truck."

Mary smiled at the wisdom of not forcing Otto home too quickly.

In the next hour, Christmas came to King of Prussia, Pennsylvania.

Life was born again in both ends of an old house.

Alexis was sleeping calmly with her mother slumped across her bed.

Otto was breathing regularly and sleeping soundly, while his brother was draped across his lower torso. Peace had come to a troubled house, and a gathering of unseen angels, unable to bewilder any shepherds in Pennsylvania, still sang their *Gloria in Excelsis Deo* so loudly that the snow stopped at last. The clouds dissolved. And Venus, a mere planet, rose in pretense as a star and took her place in the low sky to reign over the last few hours of darkness.

It was Mary who woke first. She raised her arms and twisted her shoulders to stretch out the muscles until they agreed to join her in getting out of bed. She knew Alexis was too exhausted from her long ordeal to get up early. Her eagerness to greet what Santa had brought must be postponed until her stamina would be equal to the discovery of a new coloring book. Nonetheless, Mary's first act upon rising from her temporary bed was to get the coloring book and crayons and place them under the tree. It was not a large gift to pretend that Santa had brought, but Alexis would see it as most generous and would never think of accusing Santa of being cheap. It would be a good Christmas morning.

After putting the coloring book under the tree, Mary went to the rear bedroom and smiled at the sight of a thin man in bed, breathing very

141

deeply, and his guardian hunkered over him, dissolved in rest. They were like little boys having a sleep-over. "Sleeping together after all these years," Mary whispered. She stealthily slipped out of the room and moved back into the front of the house.

Feeling a chill, she realized that in her exhaustion she had slept through the nightly burn of coal. The stove looked cold to her. Walking over to it, she opened the door and looked in. The coals gave her a little blast of warmth but only a slight one. It was time to restoke the fire. She looked at the poker and smiled at the stubby iron instrument. How odd it looked in the daylight, not at all like the Excalibur their night fears had forged into being. Her hand rammed the poker into the fire, digging at the coals until the gray ash on top swirled away leaving the fuchsia embers glowing brightly. Reaching for the coal scuttle, she was disappointed to find it empty. She picked up the black bucket and started downstairs. Determined not to wake Alexis, Mary slipped through the gloom as silently as Caspian, who watched her from the braided throw rug as though her stealth gave them something in common.

Once in the basement she went directly to the coal bin and picked up the small shovel to thrust into the coal. Lying in the swale of the shovel's blade was an envelope. Her intention of getting a scuttle of coal dissolved in her curiosity. Intrigued by the letter in the shovel's blade, she took it and dropped the shovel back into the bucket. The strong sunlight of Christmas morning flooded into the small casement window tucked beneath the upstairs floor plates. Mary walked to the window and held the letter in the bright sunshine.

Dear Mrs. Withers,

I am much afraid I will shortly be discovered and driven out of your house and perhaps arrested. I have taken this daring step only because I am destitute and needed two or three days out of the weather. I will be gone in the morning by the time you get this letter. Please accept this small pittance of money as payment for using your house as a place to stay. I am most sorry that I had not the courage to apply more formally to ask your permission. In the spirit of him who was born in a stable because the world found no place for him,

A needy friend.

Beneath the elegant writing was a gathering of bills—three twenties and three ones—sixty-three dollars! Mary was amazed at the amount. It was as if her benefactor didn't know that there were any number of small motels where he could have stayed two weeks for such a sum.

Even the old inn and tavern for which the town was named would have welcomed this amount. Now she put back together the noise she had heard on Christmas Eve, the sound of someone rattling around in the basement beneath her. How she wished she could have known that Erick's brother was her Christmas guest.

Mary stuck the envelope in her apron pocket, filled the coal bucket, and returned to the upper floor. Once again Caspian studied her. This time the added weight of the coal she carried made the floor creak loudly. She heard Alexis stirring in the next room. It was only a moment or so that the child stirred, and then she flew into the bright room and nearly tackled her mother. Her excitement over Christmas overcame her weakened state.

"Mama, is it Christmas?" cried Alexis. "Did Santa come?" she added, not waiting for an answer to her first question before she asked the second.

"It is and he did!" laughed Mary, answering both questions in a single sentence. "See for yourself, Alexis," counseled Mary. But her counsel was unnecessary. Alexis was already at the thin tree picking up the coloring book and the small box of crayons. "Oh, Mama, it's just what I wanted." The sheer wonder of it all stopped Alexis from talking, but only for a moment. "What did Santa bring you?"

"He brought me a little girl six years ago, and I haven't wanted a thing since then. Santa's very smart, Alexis. He knows that after giving me a gift as wonderful as you, no other gift could ever make me happy."

Alexis grinned at her mother. "Mama, maybe Santa wanted me to share my new coloring book with you, and we can color together all through Christmas—Mama, who's that with the coal man?"

Alexis pointed over her mother's shoulder toward the rear of the house. Mary wheeled in the direction she was pointing. There framed in the doorway stood the brothers. Erick was smiling, but Otto looked toward Mary with a plea in his eyes. He obviously wanted some nod of permission that it was all right to be there. Mary smiled, and her smile left little room for doubt that he was indeed welcome.

"Mrs. Withers, I'm afraid I must beg your forgiveness, for—"

"Otto, you are not strong enough to stand. Please sit . . . here, if you will, by the stove. It's warm here." Otto did not immediately obey her, and as he stood staring at her, Mary felt as though she was being scrutinized by a starving man. He looked so hungry she did not see how he could possibly be well. "Please, Otto," she repeated, "sit down, won't you?"

Perhaps it was because of the earnestness in

her voice that Otto, still supported by Erick, made his way closer toward the stove and took the seat Mary had designated. He did not sit in it so much as collapse on it. It was clear that life in general and his flight into the storm in particular had required nearly all the stamina he had.

"Now, don't you budge till I get you the biggest bowl of oatmeal in Pennsylvania." Suddenly Mary felt sheepish. It was Christmas morning, and all she had to offer this hungry man was a bowl of oatmeal. Erick spotted her embarrassment at having so little to offer. He could see that she was about to apologize that she had nothing else, so he quickly said, "Hey, what's this! I did all the work last night. How about making two bowls? I'll take the first one, and Otto can wait his turn."

"That's how it always was growing up, Mary. He was the baby, so he was the first to get everything," chided Otto weakly.

Mary and Erick smiled, then laughed. Otto in such a simple way had spoken and with such a perverse comment seemed to reenter the world. He had called her Mary. It was as though he was crying out to rejoin the human race.

"All right, all right! I'll be right back with coffee and oatmeal."

In fifteen minutes she came in from the rear kitchen. She had snipped some holly that grew by the back stoop and stuck it in the side of the steaming gruel. She had dyed some sugar cubes in red food coloring and nestled them in a clot of cream on top of the oatmeal. It was indeed the most festive breakfast that either of the Mueller boys could ever remember.

As Otto ate he could feel his strength return. "Mary, I must thank you for the best Christmas I've had in many years." A single drop of joy ran down across his cheek, and gratitude was as obvious as the green holly in the bottom of his empty cereal bowl.

"Now, Otto, none of that," said Mary, reaching rather awkwardly to touch his face. He ducked his eyes as if to turn from the gratitude. "This is yours, I believe," she offered, extending the sixty-three dollars.

"No, please," Otto demanded weakly yet firmly. "I cannot receive it after all the trouble I've caused you. What I did was unthinkable. And yet when my little brother was here and all things came out so gloriously, I cannot say I would have wished it otherwise. No, Mary, it will buy you coal for the rest of the winter, enough to heat your whole house at once."

"You heard him, Mary. Keep the money. It's the first decent thing I've seen the man do in twelve years. In fact, it's the *only* thing I've seen him do in twelve years." Erick smiled, and they all laughed.

In the midst of their laughter, the phone rang. It was Dr. Drummond, still snowed in at Caslin's Dairy. "How's Alexis?"

"Fine. She's just fine, Dr. Drummond." Mary interrupted their conversation a moment to wish a "Merry Christmas" to Janet and Mabel, who hung up immediately as a Yuletide gesture to Mary Withers.

"Well, if Alexis is fine, I think I'll work on getting back to town this morning. Mr. Caslin is hooking up the sleigh. It will go much better than my car this morning. I should be home in a couple of hours. Mary, please have a merry Christmas."

"It's already merry! And the same to you and Marjie, Dr. Drummond."

When the conversation was over, Erick stood up. "I think I'll borrow your coal scoop and go dig out the truck. We're all going to dine at the Muellers' today."

"No . . . no! Not Alexis and me. We'd feel so out of place. Your mother always speaks to me at church, but I'm not sure your father likes me all that well." Mary was horrified by the very idea.

"Nonsense. When Hans Mueller discovers that it was his coal in your house that provided a shelter for his son, you'll be the hero of the hour," insisted Erick.

Mary threw up her hand and started to speak

a further protest, but Erick, with some resolution, laid his index finger across her lips, sealing them with a mock gesture of finality.

Erick walked to the back of the house, where he had left his galoshes and coat after his midnight rescue and suited up. Once in the basement he grabbed the coal scoop and flew up the stairs, suddenly floating in a new lightness of being. He stepped out into an unbroken field of snow. The old truck was where he left it. He assumed it was rather in the middle of the road, although the middle, the edge, and the shoulders of the road were all indistinguishable from the fields around it. But Erick came to the truck and soon had scooped it free. He would have to guess—very carefully—where the road was situated. Fortunately the old truck sat high enough on its thick tires to avoid becoming high-centered. Swinging himself into the cab, he was not surprised to find that some of the snow had sifted inside. He brushed it off the seat, stuck the key in the ignition, and twisted. "Glory be!" he exulted as the motor roared alive. Shifting the lever, he cautiously crept down the long drive, cutting a new set of white ruts into the very white world. It felt good to pull up in front of the Witherses' house.

Now would come his first joyous act of Christmas Day. He loaded Mary and Alexis Withers, along with their surprise boarder, into the truck and headed toward the Muellers', where an eager mother and an anxious father were about to be made rich by Christmas.

Smoke rose unashamedly that day from both of Mary Withers' chimneys. The sun glittered on her white roof and on the white fields beyond. But best of all, life glittered because Erick Mueller was wedged in the narrow seat of a Chevrolet coal truck with three wonderful people who were his Christmas gift to himself. He was driving those people into his future. They were his as the day was his, and unless they all promised to make Christmas last forever, he would never let them out of that truck. King of Prussia was his kingdom, and he determined never to surrender the sway he held.

"Hans," said Ingrid, "it's in the air—can you feel it? There's something in the sunlight. It's going to be a good day, this Christmas day in the year of our Lord, 1929." Realizing she was being more dramatic than necessary, Mrs. Mueller stopped rhapsodizing, took the turkey that had been thawing during the night, filled it full of three pans of corn bread stuffing, and set the onioned-and-saged bird to bake. It was a big turkey, and Ingrid was not at all sure there would be anybody other than herself and Hans to eat it. There was still an empty large iron shelf beneath the roaster pan, begging first for the plump pies, and when they were done, the bread that would be inserted last, and Ingrid would order it to come out of the oven just at dinnertime.

But Ingrid came to nine o'clock in a terrible state of mind. She wanted her family to be together. Frustrated that after an hour and a half of clear daylight, Erick was still not home, she decided it was time to take matters into her own hands. Ingrid Mueller called the Witherses' house to see if she could entice Erick to get home the best way he could. But neither Erick nor the widow Withers were to be found. Mary Withers' phone rang and rang. Janet Breckenridge answered and so did Mabel Cartwright. But Mary Withers did not. Ingrid wondered if Mary's phone lines might be out of service due to the storm.

Now she found herself terribly frustrated. Otto might be somewhere in or around town, but she knew not where. Erick was supposed to be at the Witherses', but no one there was answering the phone. She hung up the receiver and paced before the large front window, where the Christmas tree stood squarely in the way of her view. She walked around the tree from side to side in order to position herself next to the glass. Each time she circled the tree, she huffed, audibly disappointed that Erick had not yet returned.

"Ingrid, sit down, *mein frau!*" shouted Hans. "You're making me nervous!" Hans clearly didn't like the fact that Erick wasn't home but felt that Ingrid's endless pacing would not change the situation. "Go back to the kitchen and check on the turkey."

"The turkey is fine," said Ingrid with finality.

"Vell, for goodness sake, go over the recipe for your pies."

"I don't need a recipe for pies. You think I need a recipe for pies? I don't tell you how to run a coal truck, you don't tell me how to bake pies, all right? And MERRY CHRISTMAS!"

The argument was not as cheery as Ingrid wanted Christmas to be. But there seemed no chance of their togetherness getting more cozy. Then suddenly the world changed. Just as Ingrid rounded the tree to the right side, she squeaked in joy, "Here comes the truck. Erick is on the way home. I knew he wouldn't take very long. That boy is dependable. He gets that, Hans, you know, from my side of the family. It's always been the Mueller side that dawdled."

Hans ignored the comment. He felt completely well, and Ingrid could tell it as he walked first to the window and then to the door. But it was between the window and the door that his pace brightened. His back problems were nearly over. He swung open the door, all prepared to slog, for some distance at least, through the snow. "Ingrid," he called to his wife, who had now left the window and was in the process of joining him at the door. "Vill you look at this? It's not just Erick. It's that Vithers vidow as vell. It looks like ve may be about to get a new

153

daughter-in-law for Christmas. Vhat do you think of that?"

"Well, Hans, whatever Erick wants is good enough for us too. We need to open up our family a little anyway. Who else is with Erick?"

"I can't tell, Ingrid. The vindows are too frosted ower on the inside."

There wasn't time for extra conversation. Erick was already out of the truck on the driver's side. He opened the door on the passenger side, and Mary stepped out on the running board. With some gallantry, Erick scooped her up and carried her to the porch of the house. "Papa, this is Mary Withers!" he announced.

"Ve know Mary wery vell. Merry Christmas, Mrs. Vithers!"

"And a Merry Christmas to you as well," answered Mary. "Mr. and Mrs. Mueller, I hope my daughter and I aren't intruding on your Christmas. I told Erick that this was entirely inappropriate, but he would have it no other—"

"Nor should he, my dear," Ingrid interrupted. "I can't tell you how delighted we are that you've come. You and Alexis will make our Christmas most special."

"Mama," called Alexis, who was now standing on the running board of the truck, "can I come too?" Her childish voice was like the very clear air that carried it. In hearing her beautiful and excited voice, Ingrid suddenly knew how incomplete the Muellers' Christmases had been in recent years. It takes a child to make Christmas.

Her beckoning sent Erick flying, coat opened and scarf trailing, to pick up the child. He brought her to the Mueller porch in but a moment. The Muellers were still standing there wondering why Erick had not closed the door of the truck when Otto stepped out on the running board. The sight was steeped in twelve years of waiting. So welcome it was that it spun a spell that paralyzed everyone. No one moved, but all eyes were opened to the possibility of something so wonderful, so whole that only God could measure its power.

"Papa, it's Otto!" said Otto. "I won't come in if you don't want me to. . . ."

Hans Mueller had dreamed his repentance for a dozen years, and now had come the opportunity he had asked God to provide. Now was the day when all his long-stored sorrow would at last know peace. He did not wait for Otto but began walking toward the truck. Indeed, he ran. The snow was too deep to permit it, but he did . . . stumbling, hurrying, laughing, and weeping as he ran. He fell face forward in the high snow, which only caused him to laugh all the harder. Then he rose and took two more stumbling steps.

Limping from his old war injury, Otto nearly fell off the running board as he moved from the truck toward his father. He found himself too weak to run far, but he ran as far as he could before falling exhausted in the snow.

Instantly Hans Mueller fell too. Then the coal man raised himself to one knee and lifted Otto to his feet. They embraced with such awkward passion they fell yet again in the snow.

"Father," said Otto, "forgive me!"

"Oh no, Otto. You must forgive this pigheaded old German who sinned against you so long ago. Forgive me, Otto."

With simple repentance, they held each other at arm's length and studied each other for a long moment, as though only their unbroken gaze could ensure their togetherness. Once again they embraced, kissing each other, and then, because of their exuberance and unsure standing in the uneven snow, they fell once again. Then they were laughing, sitting in nearly two feet of snow. Trying to help each other up, they fell yet again. The comedy was as healing as was the repentance, and Ingrid flew down the path to the place where both of them were sitting and laughing. But Ingrid also underestimated the depth of the snow and, being the shortest of the three, found herself unable to remain upright, stumbling and falling forward, stopping and correcting herself, once again stumbling. At last arriving to Otto, she tumbled in between Hans and Otto, finding herself on her knees in the same snow. Fully turning her back on Hans, she hugged Otto, and then Hans hugged them both. Then there were three of them sitting and laughing in the snow. Suddenly it was a repeat of 1911. They were all a family, only now they were older and wiser, but once again a family playing in the snow. Ingrid and Otto scooped up handfuls of snow and dumped them down Hans' collar. Then they all laughed again.

"Well, Mary," said Erick. "What do you say?" Erick gestured toward the rest of his fallen family who were enjoying the newness of things once lost but now repaired.

"I don't know." Mary was very tentative. "I'm really not one of the family yet, and besides, there's Alexis. Considering all she's just been through, I can't believe the snow would do her much good."

"Come here, Alexis," said Erick. The child seemed to sense this was a moment in life not to be feared. She laid her coloring book and crayons on the porch, and Erick swung her up on his shoulders. "Alexis," he asked, plenty loud enough for Hans to hear, "how would you like a German Grandpa?"

Hans quit laughing, so did Ingrid. But Erick laughed loud enough to fill up the wondering silence. "C'mon, Mary," he said, taking her hand. And the three of them walked out to the bewildered Muellers still sitting in the snow. "Welcome home, Otto!" said Erick. "Papa, this is Alexis Withers, and this is Mary Withers, whose home has long been heated by Mueller coal. She's a paying customer you know, Papa, and I for one say 'God bless her' for having a house big enough to make a place for Otto."

"Even if she didn't know I was there," said Otto with a grin.

"And in such vays God vorks his mysteries," said Hans. Reaching up for Alexis, Hans took her from Erick, who carefully handed her down to the coal man. "Alexis, you like this snow?"

"Yes, Mr. Mueller. I love snow," said Alexis shyly.

"Vell, I vill tell you after dinner about a snow ve once had in Bavaria vhen I was just about your age. The snow vas just about up to the horses' bellies and ve had to rig a cable to—"

"Papa, that Bavarian snow gets deeper every year."

"You smart-aleck kid, you think Pennsylwania has snow? I'll tell you vhat snow really is. Ingrid, ve should have raised these boys mitt more respect."

"Mary," said Erick, "*Willkommen* to the Muellers' for Christmas! Shall we?" Erick dropped to his knees in the snow with the rest of his family. Mary followed suit, and there, in King of Prussia, Pennsylvania, the elder Muellers doubled the number of their children. Old Hans smiled at Alexis, who actually wanted to hear his stories of long-ago Bavarian winters. Otto sat with his arm around Ingrid. Ingrid was overjoyed and smiled at Erick and Mary, who were holding hands; they had their gloves on, but touching is possible even with gloves on. Mary Withers knew love could root itself in winter and that snow is a clean white place to start living again.

Perhaps that was the great lesson of the storm. *The best of life's roses bud in winter*, thought Mary.

"Mama," said Alexis, "Isn't snow beautiful?"

Mary agreed. But even more beautiful was the fact that Mary and Alexis, with all four of the Muellers, were playing in the snow as if they were children.

Indeed they were. Alexis had said it well, *"We are all the children of God."*